Sagittae Angelorum

Sagittae Angelorum

Arrows of Angels; a Collection of Poetry,
Short Stories, and Drama

BY
Dominic Nootebos,
Jeremy Joosten,
Joelle Joosten, AND
Lucas Smith

EDITED BY
David C. Bellusci

RESOURCE *Publications* · Eugene, Oregon

SAGITTAE ANGELORUM
Arrows of Angels; a Collection of Poetry, Short Stories, and Drama

Resource Publications
An Imprint of Wipf and Stock Publishers
199 W. 8th Ave., Suite 3
Eugene, OR 97401

www.wipfandstock.com

PAPERBACK ISBN: 978-1-6667-8063-5
HARDCOVER ISBN: 978-1-6667-8064-2
EBOOK ISBN: 978-1-6667-8065-9

07/21/23

to those whom we love
family and friends
godchildren and godparents
living and deceased . . .

" . . . as the arrow is shot to its mark by its archer."

St. Thomas Aquinas, *Summa Theologiae*
Pt. 1, a. 2, q. 3 (5th way)

Contents

Drama—**I** (Jeremy Joosten)

Short Stories—**III** (Jeremy Joosten)

Drama—**II** (Lucas Smith)

Short Stories—**IV** (Joelle Joosten)

Short Stories—**V** (Lucas Smith)

Preface

The title, *Sagittae Angelorum,* "angel arrows" or literally, the "arrows of angels," is inspired by Aquinas's "fifth way" and serves to express this collection of literary works as "arrows" directed to their mark in poetry, drama, and short stories. Angels as with humans serve as secondary causes to carry out God's will. And humans like angels are spiritual beings; this means we have the capacity to exercise intelligence and freewill. Humans as spiritual beings are created in God's image and likeness. The highest expression of our humanness is in prayer and worship. And when we engage in creativity as embodied beings, we participate in God's creative power. *To be* human means to worship and to be creative. The most sublime form of the creative mind is to be found in language since the written word is the symbolic representation of the world. Language conveys meaning in its linguistic configuration.

The four authors of this collection bring energy and creativity to *Sagittae Angelorum.* Joelle Joosten explores spatial form and structure as part of metaphor in her poetry. Joelle examines love and suffering both in poetry and her short stories. She draws us into the powerful emotions of love and betrayal in *Turbulence;* and in her historical fiction, the intensity of music in the interior journey of Ludwig van Beethoven. Jeremy Joosten engages his readers by creating narratives with animal and nature metaphors in his poetry and short stories. The reader/listener cannot escape Jeremy's call to existential reflection on life and relationships. Jeremy achieves this personal self-examination superbly in his one-act play, *Kintsugi.* When it comes to love, Dominic Nootebos confronts his readers with the rawness of love and death in both his provocative poetry and his gothic love story, *Lost Love of the Haunted and Hollow.* Dominic also reveals a fresh playfulness in his writing where he entertains his readers in the symbols of *Duck Tavern.* Lucas Smith offers us poems where he explores with space, syntax, and images leading his reader to a spiritual ascent. Lucas's drama based on the life of Blessed Pier Giorgio Frassati encapsulates in his play the essence of the person of Pier Giorgio. Lucas ends this collection introducing his readers to Mars with his short story, *Home Bound*; and from Mars back to Earth. Lucas's sci-fi piece contains a spiritual twist that grounds his readers in reality.

David C. Bellusci, MFA, PhD, Editor

Sagittae Angelorum

Poetry

A Smile

by Jeremy Joosten

I don't know how you came to
be here.
I don't know what your purpose is.

But I do know how to find you.

At the shore,
During the sunset.
where
life with the turtles and seagulls
create a summertime bliss.
where
the sounds of the waves
are sung in rhythm of the wind

Ages ago
you were born
It shows on your skin
You look tired
But I know you are happy
Sitting there,
waiting,
At the edge of the shore.

People walk by you
Seeing nothing
but a crack
a break.

You look thrown away.
Left by the shore
Waiting to find your home.

I see
a smile,
waiting for what's coming.
bringing me closer
To see what you are.
A mouth,
calling for me to take notice
Of your strange beauty
Eager to see if I am the person
that will take you home

I see hope in her broken shell
She has conquered many feats
And lived longer than the sea
Battered and tired,

Patient and smiling.

Dying and yet living.
I sense the beauty in her,
A pearl inside

But I can't see the pearl
Without seeing her smile.
The ocean, the sunset, means nothing
Compared to the pearl of your smile.
My little pearl in peril.

"Et In Arcadia Est"

by Jeremy Joosten

On my windowsill there sits
A little plastic skull.
His name is Unimportant,
a reminder of what's passed.
Sitting there
with a very fine mustache.

He is always happy
my little plastic skull.
Grinning his pearly whites for me
Happy
when I open my eyes,
looking over me night and day
keeping me safe. Reminding me
   to smile.

His eyes glow when he's excited
a bright blue like my own
Piercing captivating electric
a light in the middle of the dark
a beacon so bright
it hurts

but still smiling,

I wonder how?

my finely mustached
Unimportant skull
you keep smiling.
Maybe you know my future.

You've seen the life I've lived
The moments of happiness.
The times of pain.
Laughing at me as I sit
Writing this poem

Because you know where I am going
how I am, who I am, who I will be.
Smiling because you know what's
   to come

To that,

I can smile with you
My little plastic skull
Knowing I will be where you
   are One Day

Sitting Unimportant
still in a windowsill
With a very fine mustache.

Bus Ride to Italy

by Jeremy Joosten

If I was on a bus to Italy
With you beside me, resting head on arm
I would dream the whole way to Sicily.
Wild, Happy, dreams of a place with no harm.
The future, with all imaginable creatures:
singing hippos or flying bears
sailing around us. Look, there's the stunning
celestial crane! And the bouncing hare!
We'd have a buffet with the stars and moon
Or we'd go trampolining on the sun
But I feel I've been dreaming much too soon
Cause on this bus, we've barely yet begun.
Perhaps, it is best not to dream, but wait
Till we reach Italy, to not be haste.

My Purple Octopus in the Bermudian Delta

by Jeremy Joosten

Oh, to breathe not in the air but in the water.
>> where I would lay among the seaweed,
>> staring at the sun,
>> nap as the seahorses gallop and giggle around my face
>> to see a sunfish up close and
>> dance with a purple octopus
>> in the middle of the Bermudian Delta.

But for what?
>> I would not be able to lie among the grass
>> not be able to stare at the sun,
>> or ride a horse.
>> I could dance with a person, and not a purple octopus.
>> But I want to be in the middle of the Delta.

>> Would I not rather breathe water than air
>> to be with You?

You make the grass and the seaweed collide, the Sun visible,
uniting the seahorse and horse as brothers.
But best of all,
in the middle of the Bermudian Delta,
You let me dance with a purple octopus.

The scale   is splitting
                              down the middle.

               "I feel pressured!" screamed the Fulcrum,
"To keep this side   . . . . . .   in harmony with that one."

                   The ends outweigh the scale itself.
                              Torn between

even-   -competitors
                              in turmoil.

                              Wait.
                              Why stress?
                              Let gravity be.

                              "Rest,
                              My little Fulcrum"
                              replied her Maker
                              "Redirect your focus."

                   Her center of gravity only,
                              she could
                              Save.

"I will let you go . . .   . . . and you my dear as well."
                   It all fell apart:
                              control.
               While the Fulcrum exchanged
                   screams for surrender:
                              her

                    Peace.

                    by Joelle Joosten

Labels or Lives

by Joelle Joosten

I have a sister who's blind . . .	. . . she reads with her fingers knows a reality unseen.
A sister chronically ill . . .	. . . she struggles in pain rows through every persistence.
And a sister paralyzed with defects . . .	. . . she does nothing, yet everything: glows of pure Love: received and given. Unconditional.

But who am I?
they call me a Teacher.

I have a teacher's heart
one that wants to give advice.
Yet I have nothing
but a wish – my dear sisters – to make your lives easier.
Instead I should thank you
for being yourselves.
My promise to walk *with* you
not to change you.

Trained for "diversity,"
textbooks taught me nothing.
I am the student of your lives,
note your Struggles *and* your Beauty.

i lost you to famine
to fire
then floods—

my bamboo house—our lavender garden—
as children we played
held safe in warm arms.
in a world of wonder,
a horizon of gold.
i kissed the Horizon,
held Your hand in mine.
troubles then are my daydreams today.
one thing went away.
then another.
till i was left to face You
and loss.

now vagabond and voyager,
i found Your Heart as my Home.

a bamboo house is simply a structure
for neighbors create our space, face-to-face.
lavender lives on
in this moment here and now
faded tomorrow and no less Sacred.
here i find myself

Lost in a Voyage of You

by Joelle Joosten

Duck Tavern

by Dominic Nootebos

The tired wanderer,
after a perilous search,
found a stroke of luck.
He came upon a humble tavern,
and to his surprise,
it was filled with ducks.

"What," he said,
with confusion and annoyance.
"Quack Quack," said the bartender,
plain and simply,
and poured him a cup of ale
with grace and splendour.

The wanderer sat down,
grunted, then looked around.
Bread gambling at this corner,
an indoor pond in another,
quacks and alcohol all around—
no place for a foreigner.

And the ducks sang their duck songs,
filling the tavern
with a drunk cacophony of quacks.
Joyful merriment
and breadcrumb banqueting ensued,
until a hooded duck cleared his throat in the back.

Tension filled the tavern,
all ducks motionless,
not a single one made a sound.
The hooded duck rose from his chair,
gave a menacing "quack,"
and complete chaos spread abound.

The tavern turned into a tempest of quacks,
tables, bread, and drinks thrown about,
ducks waddling furiously to and fro,
while the hooded duck stood cackling in the midst.
The wanderer took a sip of ale then stood,
and cupped the hooded duck in his hands like a wad of dough.

He strode outside,
placed the menace down,
patted his head,
watched him waddle away,
then retired to his room
and went to bed.

Now the ducks tell the tale
of the heroic wanderer
that came on that fateful day.
They feast in his name
and sing the song
of the man who put the storm at bay.

A Painful Encounter for the Lonely

by Dominic Nootebos

The man sat on the crowded bus,
a steady pour of rain.
Gazing out with lifeless eyes,
pondering the life he disdains.

Checked off a day of grudging work;
a monotonous, meaningless grind.
Rotting away before keyboard and screen,
motivation growing harder to find.

The bus hisses and he meanders out,
another umbrella in the sea;
drifting down the river of sheep
when he heard a distant cry of glee.

His attention turned to a small charming park,
a spot from his distant past.
He sat himself down on the now peeling bench,
bygone memories beginning to amass.

He placed a cold hand on the lovers' engraving,
lost in an earlier time.
A constant patter of rain on his umbrella;
so far from his former prime.

Suddenly he heard the distant cry once again,
and spotted that familiar face.
A small child sprang out from behind her mother,
splashing water all over the place.

A mix of emotions all in an instant:
beauty, bitterness, shock.
Shrinking down, he let them pass by;
no desire to talk.

He sat frozen for a moment, festering inside,
thinking of what could have been.
He then picked himself up and hardened his heart;
a painful struggle unseen.

Now at home, sitting alone,
telling himself he's okay.
Awake in bed with this never ending rain,
awaiting yet another day.

Lying in the Sun

by Lucas Smith

my attention is torn asunder
   despite the beauty of a spring day
   even when beneath an oak I lay
   my mind puts this sight under
the branches sway like a dancer
   when caught by a gust, they play
   and when it is past, they stay
   but still my sight is stolen by Her
as elegant as the softest willow
   Her love as vast as a field
   a smile like a mid-spring sun
the complexation of the daises yellow
   a voice so sweet and mild
   it is Her who has my thoughts in stun

Stepping out into a Field

by Lucas Smith

to gaze upon a sunset
is to await the stars.
One gives way for many—
sacrifice for all

each placed—
arrayed in symphony.
impossible chaos
ordered exactly

some claim names:
Vela, Orion, Aries, Ara—
formed for us
in the beginning . . .

the Cosmic Cathedral,
grandeur beyond
but here,
silence.

left standing
mind
detached
floating with Andromeda

tossed to Cassiopeia
a discussion with Corvus
battle against Draco
humbled by Leo.

descend—
cool damp grass
tear in eye,
heart cries out

who am i so small
cut at the heart—
ministered by this orchestra
here i am Lord.

Upon Awaking in the Morning

by Lucas Smith

I find myself buried
by blankets
I am sinking
into the dirt of
comfort

I must arise!
I must see
the sunrise!
O but to wake
to see it glow!

Darkness met my
thoughts

If you but lie down
once more
this and more
will fill your dreams

I do not want your
allusion O Dark!
You play tricks in my mind
but I shall like to see
with my eyes!

I throw off the
coffin of fluff,
step on to the cold
floor

I shuffle towards
curtains
I invite in the day
to dispel
the Darkness.

Sagittae Angelorum

Short Stories—I

Turbulence

by Joelle Joosten

Vroom, vroom.

Easily distracted by what was beyond her kitchen window, Katie re-gathered enough attention for washing the dishes again. She was curious about a plane that had flown overhead. It made her dream of happier days. When she was young, and in love, and life was simpler. If she were up in that plane, Katie would have heard a warning from the captain,

"Attention all passengers. We are experiencing a bit of turbulence. Please fasten your seatbelts."

Realizing that a dry sponge was in her hand, Katie wondered how long she had been staring out that window.

Buzz interrupted her phone. So much for the dishes. The text read, "I will be there in a second, sweetie," with a kissing emoji.

A second!? She hurried to get herself together. The kitchen still had to look somewhat decent. When he walked in, Katie ran and gave him a hug. The man spun her around with a big kiss on the lips.

"Now, about that paperwork." He winked.

"Yes." She nervously tightened her hair to her scalp then rung out her fingers.

"Sweetie, calm down. Your husband isn't here."

She nodded.

"And wow! Does your kitchen always look like an animal went through it? I knew you were struggling with mental health, Katie, but ha—this mess is even more than I can handle."

She looked down at the floor and bit her lip.

"Hey, I'm just joking around. Don't take things so personally all the time. I am a nice guy, remember? I will help you clean up and then we can get back to business." He swung Katie around and made out with her again. She loosened up a bit.

At least someone is here to help me.

They seemed to lose track of time.

Thud. Car keys were dropped on a stack of paperwork as if to say, "THIS IS MY HOUSE!"

Startled, they looked up to find that a third person had joined their party. It was Katie's husband dead silent, his face turning all sorts of colors.

"Bunny," whispered Sam, confused and forlorn.

"Sam!" Katie let out a deep sigh and covered her face.

"Welp! This is awkward." Her friend jumped from the table. "I think I overstayed my welcome. Goodbye sweetie . . . orrr . . . I mean Katie. Nice meeting you Sam." He patted him on the back—more like a desperate punch to look playful—and ran out with the door slamming behind him. There was a loud echoing in the street like a sonic boom. Sam wondered if the sound would ever end.

"Katie? What is this about?"

"Paperwork."

"Yeah, that's what it looks like but don't take me for a fool, Katie.

"I—I, *ahum,*" she coughed to clear her voice. "I didn't know you would come home so early . . . You see, you're rarely ever home . . . and I uh," she swallowed hard, " . . . I am very sorry."

"How long have you two been together?" Asked her husband.

Katie hunched her back, her posture tightened with shoulders to her ears. "Look, Sam. I was falling behind at work and Ken would come over to our house from time to time to help me keep up. He's nice like that. What is so hard to understand? And like any nice guy, he has a dog. Its name is Spot. I saw him the other day and we played fetch. You would probably like Spot . . . "

"Katie, you're rambling. This isn't the full story; I know what I saw. How long have you two been seeing each other?"

"Only recently." She shrugged and avoided eye contact.

"Recently? Like how recently? A few weeks?"

"More than that," she muttered.

"A few months?"

"A year. A year, Sam. There's your answer!"

Sam was too shell-shocked to say anything now. The door slamming seemed to continue its echo from the street corners and back into his ears.

"Sam. Wait—"

Enough was enough. Sam needed some space to breathe. To process. To clear his head. Sam's feet kept going, he didn't want them to stop.

He could walk on forever. Houses passed by, cheering children, mothers calling them in for dinner. But none of that mattered. One faded away after another. Moments disappearing into thin air, his feet still hitting the rough ground.

Then there was a familiar park bench on the top of a grassy-green hill. From Sam's perspective it faced a wall, but he knew there was an ocean on the other side. The hill looked steep, and for that reason he felt it calling his name. He needed something beautiful, and the threat of the hill looked exhilarating. One foot in front of the other. A steady march. The ocean was peaking its gentle head above the wall, till Sam reached the bench, and he saw that it went on forever.

Quiet. Stillness.

Sam took in a deep breath as he sat down. He stared out at the beautiful blue ocean with no concept of time, watching the sun set. Katie would often share this park bench with him, it was their favorite lookout. Maybe he just needed to see her face again. From this distance.

Would that help calm me down? For now, at least. Maybe.

Sam retrieved his wallet and pulled out a photograph. Two smiling faces. His first time in the pilot seat. Katie next to him, radiant with joy. She was the flight attendant. Their first time flying together. Oh, sweet memories of happier days. Then she had to work at the law firm instead.

Who is this Ken, anyway? Wondered Sam. *Was our love just a passing moment? Is this photograph meaningless? No! Some things are meant to last.*

Sam flipped over the picture. On the back it read, "Katie and Sam: The sky's our limit." The inscription below read the date of their wedding day.

He hunched over and covered his face, all alone in the open air. Choking on his tears. *How could God allow this to happen?* Sam thought their little family was perfect. *Who was I kidding? I am such a daydreamer. Maybe I saw the world through a childish lens until now.*

On an impulse, Sam ripped their photo in half. Her smile on the cement, his smile confined again to its wallet. There came a temptation to stomp on her face as well, but Sam thought it better to distract himself. The ocean was a calmer sight, the ocean was whole. He sat there meditating well after sunset, lost in its silent embrace.

"Lord, help me carry this cross!" Sam cried out.

The night was darkening, and eventually he had to fumble his way back home, tired, and exhausted. Katie's half of the photograph was left behind, suspended in time.

Ring, ring, ring,

chimed the school bell with no moment to lose. The classroom doors swung open, excited children chanting their freedom from every corner. Balls bouncing, taggers chasing, who will win slide castle?—and in the middle of this chaos, one quiet boy stretched out his arms on either side. *Vroom vroom*, he was an airplane with nothing but the sky as his limit. Running in circles, his legs were the engine, his quivering lips the propeller, and his arms the wings that allowed him to fly.

One curious girl lost her game of slide castle, and seeing the boy, marched right up to him with hands on hips.

"Do you always play by yourself at wecess?

"Wecess?" Asked the boy.

She became exasperated. "W-ee-cess." The girl said again, this time waving her hands in the air as if pointing to everything explained what she was trying to say.

"Oh recess." The boy understood. "Yes, I quite like playing by myself. But you can join if you want to. We can be friends."

"Okay. But if we're going to be friends, don't ask me to say the word, 'Wabbit.'" To express what she meant, the girl made long ears atop her head with her hands and stuck out her only two adult teeth to make a rabbit face.

"I won't," replied the boy." We don't talk about rabbits. I will say 'bunny' instead."

The girl became more curious. "So, you don't think I speak funny?"

"No, not at all."

Her posture eased and a smile spread from ear to ear.

"My name is Katie."

"Mine is Sam."

They spread out their arms together. Now there were two airplanes flying on the playground. Their half-toothy grins sparkled in the sunlight.

Vroom vroom. Vroom vroom.

"Where are we going Sam?" she hollered above the wind in their ears.

"The sky's our limit, Katie."

Beeeep, beeeep. Beeeep, beeeep,

screeched an angry alarm clock. Sam looked suspiciously calm at the kitchen table. Coffee in one hand, newspaper in the other. The title on his newspaper read, "Dubai Plane Collision."

Katie had just awakened. Her eyes fluttered to the ground, and she forgot all about her plan to make coffee for herself. Katie then saw that the floor needed to be vacuumed. *Yes, that would be a good distraction,* she thought.

"Bunny," his soft voice made its way over the menacing vacuum. She had to turn it off. "Did you hear about the planes that clipped one another on a taxiway?"

Katie barely shook her head no; her mind was wandering somewhere else. And just as Sam had intended, she got the conversation started.

"You know Sam, I've been thinking."

"You've been thinking. Okay."

"I don't think things are working out for us."

"Really?"

"You're always gone. You leave me to do the dishes. When you are home from work, you always have something else to do. You spend more time with your friends than with me."

Confused about where all these accusations were coming from, he responded with, "I am an airline pilot. I cannot help my schedule or change where I am supposed to be. It's my job. I didn't realize you felt this way. Why didn't you say anything earlier?"

"I thought you'd know. I mean, we barely see one another. It's kind of obvious."

"What are you talking about?"

"Well for example, I was so excited to celebrate your birthday with you a few months ago. I had a whole surprise planned. We were going to eat out and then at the last second, you made plans with your friends. You came home late. I had to cancel the reservation."

"Well, how was I supposed to know that? Had I known that I wouldn't have gone. And, again, you didn't tell me till right now."

"It was a surprise. And then this other time—"

"—And how does that make doing what you did okay? How does that help anything?"

"You're turning this on me? Honey, you know my mom is terminally ill. It's weighing down on my mental health. I am doing everything I can to help her. And I still must maintain a job. You get to fly around in the sky. Well guess what? I don't get to do that anymore. I miss being a flight attendant! I had to change jobs so it would be easier to take care of my mom. I did not choose it. I don't even like being a secretary at the law firm anyway! I have too many things to manage. It's so stressful! It is not even fair! I come home from work, the house is a mess, and you're not even present here to support me. How do you think that makes me feel?"

"I guess I suck more than I thought I did. I am so sorry Kathrine Marie, I did not mean to hurt you. I say this with all the sincerity of my heart. But explain this to me: How does that give reason for your douche bag friend coming into my house behind my back? For a whole year! What were you hoping to do Katie? What were you hoping to do?" Sam's tone was becoming intense. Not typical to his gentle nature. His words hung in the air like thick icicles ready to drop.

"Look Sam," she yelled back, "I am doing everything I can for my mom, but I cannot help her if I don't put myself first. Everything I do is to love her, but I do not even feel loved myself. Do you know what that feels like? You do not support me in my struggles. I've been so lonely. My friend who you call a douche bag, he's actually nice. Sure, you caught us making out. But he understands my situation and helps me keep up with work. Why do you have to make everything about you?"

"I'm not! I was making it about us until you made it about you!"

"Okay Sam. Look. I love you and all. But sometimes things don't last. We've had good memories together. I am going to treasure them for the rest of my life, but relationships are like nature. Nature has beautiful flowers and animals, but they all come to pass. Nature evolves and things change. It's like that. We lost our spark and now it's time to move on. I think you should too."

"Don't you start with that! This isn't a highschool date you can just drop with some fluttery words and no harm done. That's bullshit! "

"Okay." Katie pursed her lips and blinked back tears. She gave up talking.

"We are not giving up on us! I am NOT giving up on us! For better or for worse, right? That meant something to me, and I know it meant something to you."

Without a word, Katie went back to the vacuum. *Click*, she turned the switch on.

Click, click,

the airplane doors closed, wheels unlocked, all passengers and compartments readied for takeoff. With her fancy scarf and heels, Katie walked down the aisle to double check everything. Most flight attendants are chipper on commercial airlines, but she had a different energy. There was an authenticity in her excitement; in the way she walked and the certainty of her posture. This was the first time Sam had ever flown a plane. And it was with her! Everything was perfect. How did she get so lucky as to be with him on this first adventure?

The flight went smooth overall, well, minus a bit of turbulence. He hit the ground rough, and all the passengers were in a fright, but Katie was there to encourage Sam.

"You got this, Love. Your next flight will be better. The hard part is over, and you can only do better from here. The sky's our limit, right?"

"The sky's our limit. Thanks, Bunny."

Bing. "Yay," the cheerful noise of passengers freed at last. They went out single file. Katie had her arm around Sam as he sat in the pilot's seat. She watched them leave one by one, very proud of their successful journey.

"Thank you for flying with us. Have a good day. Thank you for flying with us. Have a good day." She repeated this for each passenger.

As Sam sat there, his palms were sweating. He listened to the steady beat of her voice as if it were a metronome. It helped to calm his nerves. The people seemed to drag on forever. He felt for a little box in his pocket. *Good. Still there. It's almost time now. So many people. Just listen to the metronome. Listen to the metronome.*

She reached her last, "Have a good day." All crew eyes were on him, for everyone but Katie knew what would happen next.

Sam got down on one knee. "Katherine Marie, will you marry me."

"Yes! A thousand times yes!"

How could anything go wrong? Thought Katie. *I've found my Prince Charming.* They reached the sky together; everything seemed perfect.

Flip, flip,

27

went the pages of Sam's Bible as he searched for his favorite verse. Its thin pages echoed into the empty void of his seemingly one-person apartment.

"I can do all things through Christ who strengthens me." He read over and over to himself. It became the steady beat to a music of silence...

Where was Katie? How many days has she been gone?

After prayer, Sam felt unnaturally weary, but gathered enough energy to pick up his laptop. The blue light reflected a sickly glow onto his unshaven face. *Bah-bing*, chimed the website to notify Sam that his order was placed. Then he noticed the phone ominously staring back at him. Should he call? *Yes. No. Best not to have regrets.* He picked it up before his mind would change. *Ring ring.*

She picked up! Wow, what a surprise.

"Well look who it is," grumbled Katie's mom, unenthused. *Cough, Cough.* "What do you want?" Her voice was getting raspy. A twinge of pain flickered in Sam's heart as he listened to her hacking her lungs out. He wished he could do more to help her.

"Yes, um," he swallowed hard. "You know. I am calling like I do every week to let you know that the take-out food I ordered for you is on its way."

"It's about time!"

"And I ordered an extra serving, just in case."

"In case of what? You want me to die already? I see, you want to make me happy. Just in case my time will come sooner than expected." She had a morbid sense of humor. Thankfully, Sam knew that about her, or he would have taken her comment the wrong way. Another coughing fit came to swallow up any attempt of her laughing.

Sam waited for it to pass.

"What do you want now?" No humor this time. "Why haven't you hung up yet?"

"Well, I sent the extra serving in case Katie would be there. She's with you, right?"

"Wouldn't you like to know."

"Tell Katie that no matter how great the turbulence, I will not give up on us. She will know what I mean."

"Oh, you haven't heard? She hasn't told you?" rasped her voice.

"Heard what?"

"She filed for divorce papers. They are coming in the mail right now. I thought you knew."

Thud. Sam dropped the phone.

How did it come to this?

He stopped talking, forgot he was even in the middle of a conversation. In lieu of his absence, Katie's mom gladly hung up the phone. He fell on the couch and bawled his eyes out like a baby. *I need to get out. I need to run.*

Suddenly he was behind the steering wheel. How did he get there? Sam had no idea. For a quick second, he had a glimpse of a neighbor's kid playing in the grass with a toy plane in his hand. But just like that, the child was gone, and Sam thought nothing of him. Another passing moment. Open road ahead. If he weren't driving so fast, Sam would have watched the child soar his plane high into the sky *vroom, vroom.* So graceful, so elegant. Then suddenly, *boom!* It turned upside down and face-planted into the ground. Fiery explosion. An awful accident.

Sam drove onwards. Trees passing by. *Whoosh, whoosh.* Faster and faster, they went. Not a care in the world. Only a man, free on the open road. Why was he driving again? *It doesn't even matter.* Sam reminded himself. The trees were gone now, the city behind. Only open space. Where was he at now? Sam could no longer recognize the place he grew up. His mind was too far gone. *What is life? Some things must matter, right?* Tears swelled up in his eyes. There was the steering wheel and the seat. Holding him. Safe in his existence. The only support left.

The yellow line blurred. *HONK!!!* Warned an angry truck. *Which is the brake pedal? Which is the gas?* Sam could not remember.

It was too late.

Everything happened so fast.

There was a loud ringing in Sam's ears. He was too delirious to feel his head go through the car window. There were pretty colors. Like stained glass windows on a beautiful sunny day. *Can you hear the church bells ringing? A glorious anthem for the bride and groom.*

A figure was walking towards him.

"Sir! Are you all right? Are you all right? Can you hear me? Sir?"

The man was wearing white, but Sam saw his beautiful bride.

Katie. Radiant. All a glow. Ready to start their new lives together.

The organ chanted its glorious ceremony, the choir singing. Sirens screaming.

Then, the awaited words:

Katie's voice glistened above the panicked sirens. "I, Katherine Marie, take you, Sam, to be my lawfully wedded husband, to have and to hold from this day forward, for better or for worse, for richer, for poorer, in sickness and in health . . . "

"I got the stretcher," a rude voice interrupted Sam's scattered thought. *What stretcher? This is my wedding day.* His body was being moved about but he could not move. The lights were pretty. Red and white. Red and white, like the altar colors.

" . . . from this day forward until death do us part," she was so beautiful. *I will do anything for her.*

Crackle, crackle,

Katie watched the fire dance. It was so mesmerizing, so calming. She had a hot chocolate in her hand and a blanket around her shoulders. Her mother put down a phone call, and a coughing fit interrupted Katie's short-lived peace.

"I got you mama. You're all right." She put down her hot chocolate and went to the kitchen to grab her a glass of water.

"There you go," she whispered gently. Katie brushed out her mother's hair and put it up in braids. "You are so beautiful."

"Beautiful? You must be blind, honey. It's not like I'm on my death bed or anything." She reminded herself not to laugh this time, for fear that another coughing fit would come.

"You are beautiful to me. You have always been beautiful to me." Katie kissed her on her gray forehead.

Her mom let out a deep sigh.

"What's wrong?"

"I would not be here if it weren't for your wretched father."

"Yes mama, I know. You blame him for everything."

"When he left us, I had to raise you children on my own and smoking was the only comfort I had. But I would not change my habits. Self-care is important Katie. I had to comfort myself first so I could comfort you."

"And in return, I would do anything for you, mama."

"I know you would."

Katie started crying.

"What's wrong darling?"

"Love hurts."

"It does." *Cough, cough, cough.*

Katie started talking. She didn't wait for the coughing fit to end because it was more to process her own emotions than to tell her mother. "Love should make us happy, right? But for some reason happiness doesn't last. Sam should know by now that we lost our spark. He doesn't seem to get it. He keeps telling me that we made a vow. And I agree with him, we did. But 'vow,' is such an old-fashioned word. It's too much pressure to put on someone who's hurting. This is the 21st century. He's way too traditional. I thought love was about being happy; I do not feel like we are happy together like we used to be."

Her fit was over. She put a weak arm over Katie's shoulder. "All I want is for you to be happy Katie."

"But mama! I've never known what it's like to be happy. Dad left when I was just a baby. Life has not been fair to me! And soon I will lose you. Sam is just like dad. He's not around to support me. How could his pilot job be more important? Seems like it makes no difference to him whether I am a flight attendant or not. He still seems happy. Well guess what? It's makes no difference to me whether he's home or not, either!"

"But you have good friends, right? What about that lad you talk about? The one who supports you with your new job?" She inquired with her tender raspy voice.

"He's nice."

"Is he really?"

"Of course. Why do you ask?"

"Katie, I know you all too well. You haven't been yourself lately. You try to be strong. You keep silent to pretend like nothing is bothering you, but everything is expressed through your body language. I noticed you've been carrying yourself differently. For about a year now, maybe."

"How so?"

"You are terribly stiff, and you were not before. You constantly clean. More than usual, I mean. You're always fixing every tiny hair on your head. If one is out of place, you'll look imperfect it seems. You do not move like you're free anymore. Katie, is he a nice friend to you?"

"In all honesty, no." She moved her shoulders up to her ears and took in a deep breath. This was the first time she admitted that to herself. Mothers know everything, unfortunately.

"I thought Ken was nice. I only intended for us to be friends. I did not imagine things would go this far. My life has been such a disaster lately. I try to do everything to help you, to keep up with the law firm, my house, and to take care of myself—it's too much. I don't think I am handling stress well. I'm also depressed, and I don't know why. When we first met, he would remind me that I am beautiful. I missed hearing that from a man. It made me feel like my life was not as much of a mess as I thought it was, that I can do anything, that I am capable. But he is not so nice anymore. A week ago, he looked at my kitchen and made fun of my mental health. Told me that an animal must have gone through it, and he didn't realize I was this much of a mess. And that is only part of the story. Ken is not who I thought he was. Now I just feel used."

"I did not intend to betray Sam. Things just happened. Ken was so friendly at first, but our relationship turned into something else. But in my defense, I feel like Sam forgot about me. When I was new to the law firm, I missed Sam terribly. I would look for him everywhere, in people and in little moments that would remind me of him. Then, I just got used to his absence. I got used to feeling abandoned. Seems to be the story of my life, anyway. I do not think he missed me half as much as I did him. When he was home, he would spend time with his friends, and not with me. I miss the good old days, when we still had our spark, and we would fly in the sky together. I miss being a flight attendant! I used to feel so free. But now I am so alone. Maybe I am right to start the divorce process or maybe I screwed up. I am not sure. I feel so ashamed. But I cannot face him. That's why I am trying to move on. But as always, I am left feeling unloved. I do not know why Sam and I lost our spark. Meanwhile, Mr. Nice-guy treats me like shit. I just want to start over. Start a new life, all afresh."

Ding Dong. The doorbell went off.

"Oh, were you expecting guests, mom?"

"No, it's our dinner. Can you be a darling and get the door for me? The couch ate me. I can't move."

"Of course." Katie retrieved the food. "Mama, I didn't know you ordered take-out. How did you know this is my favorite dish?"

"I didn't. Sam ordered it for us."

"Sam!?"

"He sends me food every week."

"He does!?"

"Honey, if I had a man like your husband I would be set for life."

I didn't know he still cared that much. Katie was speechless.

"Excuse me mama, I am going to go outside for a minute." She needed some fresh air, maybe a new perspective as well. Katie made sure to take the food with her.

As she stepped outside her mother's house, the setting sun captured Katie's attention. There was a plane flying in its direction. The sun was moving behind her favorite hill and to one side of it was a wall that blocked her view of the ocean. The wall was there for the city's transit system. *Choo choo,* she could hear it moving on the other side, probably carrying passengers home. Sam used to order this meal for them all the time. Then, they would sit atop the hill so they could eat while the setting sun turned the ocean to all sorts of warm colors like a dance that never ended. Careful not to spill her food, Katie climbed to the top. She imagined Sam next to her like the sweet days when they were happy. If only things were still like that. Her heart felt heavy, and she ate her take-out alone.

The wind started to play with her hair, and with it came a small weather-beaten paper. A new curiosity arose from her sadness, and Katie delicately snatched the poor thing before it flew away. She unraveled it, careful that it wouldn't fall apart. There she found a familiar face; her face, smiling back at her. Katie recognized the flight attendant scarf. The colors of the photograph had faded a bit, but she knew the background was a cockpit. This felt so long ago, like a memory from another world. Katie couldn't look away, her eyes transfixed to the poor beautiful thing. She then noticed that her younger self was showing off a new ring.

Oh yes! This was the day Sam proposed to me.

"But how did you make your way to me?" she whispered to the photograph. Something was clearly missing. One end was torn off. Sam was gone.

She turned over the paper, and on the other side was half their phrase: " . . . our limit."

Isn't this the picture Sam carries in his wallet? Of course, my half has been left here to rot. But alas, everything comes to an end, right?

Katie decided to cherish memories and move on from the difficult ones.

I've felt abandoned for most of my life, even in marriage. Maybe just like this picture, life is better on my own. I will be my own happiness from now on. I don't need a man to make me happy.

With that, she decided not to feel bad if Sam was still stuck on his vow. The divorce papers were on their way.

Ring, ring. Katie nearly fell off the bench and spilled her favorite food. She wasn't expecting a call so late.

"Yes?"

"Is this Sam's wife?"

"Was his wife, is his wife, I don't know anymore. Who's asking?"

"This is Saint Joseph's hospital, mam. He's been in a terrible car crash; I think you should come and see him."

Beep.
Beep.
Beep.

Sam's eyes were closed but a sliver of white was left open like his half-ajar mouth. His lips were more of a pale blue and his face was left gray and blotchy from the accident. This color, plus the bruises surrounding his eyes made him resemble a racoon. Sam looked worse than death. Katie was glad there was a heart monitor in the hospital room because the state she found Sam in made her heart stop. At least his was still going.

That was the moment Katie realized she did not want to lose Sam. But it was too late. *What if he never opens his eyes again? I need to ask Sam's forgiveness.*

Grief's gravity hit Katie physically. The white hospital floor fell from her feet like a great black hole from outer space. She was falling. Katie became very disoriented. She looked down and was surprised to see that the floor was still there in one piece. It was like her eyes were deceiving her because after checking, she still felt her body falling. Katie's perception of life must have been swallowing her whole, turning things upside down. *Will Sam ever wake up?* Was all Katie could think. She fell

down,

down,

down,

some unknown tunnel like the artery of a heart. And when it stopped, where was she? Someone must have turned the lights off. Everything was dark. At least Katie felt something beneath her. *Why is the ground sticky?* Katie squinted in the darkness and made out a sort of tar-like substance all over her body. It was thick and sticky, stronger than glue. Katie tried to recall the last events to reorient herself. She got to the hospital as fast as she could after receiving the phone call. But alas, it was too late to think about horrible things. The tar was warm. Maybe she could take comfort in it and get some rest.

Chirp chirp, the sun started to shine through the hospital window. Days could have passed. Weeks? Months? Katie had no idea; time acted weird. *It's only a dream. Only a dream.* Katie opened one eye slowly, and then the other. She still found herself in the tar pit. Katie screamed.

"Someone! Help me! I'm stuck." She yelled three times. Desperate, wondering if anyone saw her in her situation. Then a hand gently rested on Katie's back.

"Do not be afraid darling, I'm here." Katie was unable to turn over. Firmly planted, all she could see was the tar in front of her face. Belly down, forearms keeping her supported so her head would not sink.

"Mama? Is that you"

"Yes," delighted to comfort her daughter. No coughing attack, not even the slightest wheeze that Katie knew as a child.

Katie felt her mother's fingers pick at the tar on her right hand and then up her arm. As her mother peeled away, Katie's skin came off with it. The sensation hurt terribly but it made her arm free. It was also satisfying in some odd way, like a reptile shedding its old layer of skin. Katie was bound by so much sadness and sin that she had not experienced such freedom in a long time.

"Your turn now my beautiful girl."

Rip.

Rip.

Rip.

Katie went at it for days, one painful bit at a time till every square inch-of her body renewed.

Now she could turn around and see her mother.

"Mama. Where are you?"

The voice took on a different form. Of some unseeable presence that was holding and sustaining her into existence. Katie felt an embrace, not a physical one, but one that hugged the core of her very being. An embrace that loved every aspect of who she is.

"Who are you?" She asked the voice, squinting into the abyss.

"I am."

Katie looked around for the first time. She saw a hill, the hill where she had received the hospital call. Only, it was not the hill, but something that resembled it. The ocean was fully visible with no wall to conceal it, with great depths of blue that could cover the depths and breadth of the whole world. Katie stood up to find that gravity had no hold on her feet. She seemed to be floating above the ground. Katie ran and pranced and jumped, like an excited child on the moon who just learned to walk. Flowers everywhere, one for every hue in existence sang to the tune of her dancing steps.

Then, Katie looked at herself to find no tar. Her hands were small and chubby. Then she felt her face and it was also small and chubby. Two large teeth stuck out of Katie's smile like a rabbit and sparkled in the gentle sunlight. Then she looked down. *Oh! My feet are so cute!* Katie wiggled her tiny toes, and the grass joined the flowers in harmony.

"You made me into a child again!" She cried and raised her eyes to the sky.

I thought I was removing tar. My skin came with it too and removed years from my life. Kathrine Marie was shining and radiant again with the beauty of an innocent child.

Vroom,

vroom,

vroom.

She heard a little boy's voice echoing from on top of the hill. She ran to Sam and with each step the flowers sang,

beep

beep

beep.

She ran up the hill to the rhythm, one foot for each *beep*. Then she found the little boy, but his song was not as happy as the beauty surrounding them. He sat in the grass crying, his arms on either side of him like a wilted cross.

"What's wrong Sam?"

"I broke my leg and cannot fly." He flapped both arms to show them as airplane wings. But unable to run on his own, he could not gather lift for his flight.

"We can fly together."

"How would we do that?" asked little Sam puzzled.

"Here, put your arm around my shoulders. I'll help you stand." Katie took hold of him and helped Sam up. Two little chubby arms holding one another.

He rose on one leg. "Ready?" She asked.

"Ready."

Katie walked them around in a circle so their flight could gain momentum and Sam hopped along. The hopping turned into a run. Their feet lifted higher and higher.

"*Vroom Vroom*," the wind kissed Sam's tears away.

"We are doing it! We're really flying!"

"We made it Sam!" The air was filled with the laughter of little children.

"It's like we always said Bunny, 'the sky's our limit.'"

Their laughter chirped around them and echoed into the neverending sky, like little chicks who found their wings. Traveling high and low, their echoes stirred the ocean below who in response, waved its blue current back at the happy flying couple. They flew higher and higher, two children—arm in arm— in the open air, till the clouds too were below with stars all around. *This must be what it's like to be free.* They continued onwards through time and space. Then Katie found herself traveling up a tube like the artery of a heart.

Knock. Knock.

"I am here to remind you that physical therapy is in five minutes. Is Sam awake?"

"No, I will wake him." Katie replied to the hospital nurse, who nodded and disappeared to her next duty.

Katie reached for Sam's hand on the hospital bed. His skin was noticeably vibrant compared to the day of the accident. There were still purple and yellow bruises around his eyes that were fading away slowly.

"Good morning, love."

Sam looked around alert, woken up from an exhausted sleep.

"You're here?"

"Of course, I am."

"You don't . . . have to stay . . . Bunny, with me." Full sentences were a struggle for him.

"How's that?" Katie choked on her tears. *I tried so long to reconcile myself with God, how could he say such a thing?*

"Look at me!" Sam's confined breaths filled the small hospital room, his face turned to red and his eyes watered. Strangely, Sam's body did not move in sync to express these depths of inward despair. He was paralyzed from the neck down.

"Sorry."

"Sorry about what Sam?"

"I might . . . hold you back."

"No Sam! I am the one who should apologize." A sob erupted from her throat that could be heard down the hospital corridor. Then Katie gathered enough composure to finish her thought. This was the first full conversation she had with Sam in too long. "I am sorry for what I did to you. I am sorry about the accident. I am sorry about so many things. You don't deserve any of it. I wish I could go back in time—"

Katie felt Sam's fingers in her hand twitch, as if he willed his hand to give some sort of forgiving gesture towards her. He looked her in the eyes, relived by her presence.

"Now I can . . . spend all . . . time." The corners of his lips moved up slightly. Katie laughed for both; her eyes still wet from crying. Now the hospital corridor experienced a sense of comedy. Sam was making a joke out of her original argument that he had not spent enough time with her. Now given the slow recovery, all they had was time; time to heal, time to forgive, and time to love.

"Here, I will help you to physical therapy. I was told once while you were sleeping that you should be able to gain most of your mobility back. The doctors do not think your paralysis is a chronic condition," explained Katie.

The nurse came in, right on cue. She helped Sam get his arm around Katie's shoulders. With one on either side, they helped him stand from the bed.

Sam arose on one leg with most of his body weight leaning on them, "Ready?" Katie asked.

"Ready."

They sat him in a wheelchair. "Kathrine Marie?" His eyes were filled with many words. *How will we manage*? Sam wanted to ask.

Katie knew Sam's thoughts by the expression on his face. "This is like that time you first landed a plane. You gave me such a fright, not to mention our scared passengers."

Sam chuckled.

"But then you eventually learned how to land smoothly. This is the same thing. You will learn to walk again. I promise. The sky is our limit."

"No limit," Sam replied.

"That's right," said Katie.

She wheeled him out his hospital room and they went off to therapy. Katie and Sam left broken, but they left broken together. On the small hospital desk by his bed were two pictures. One was of Katie's mother—may she rest in peace—and the other was the engagement photograph Sam would carry around in his wallet. The two halves were taped back together. Sam's side recovering from the tare, Katie's side weather-beaten and faded. On the back, their phrase was renewed, "The sky's our limit," and below it, the inscription of their wedding date.

Sagittae Angelorum

Short stories—II

Lost Love of the Haunted and Hollow

by Dominic Nootebos

I'll never forget that wistful night. Sitting in the piano room with drink in hand, thinking of my beloved Alice once again, wishing if I could only see her once more . . . Our house had never felt more cold or empty that night. But then as if by some blessing or curse—I do not know which—I saw her.

She was sitting at the windowsill, gazing out at the waning moon. The faintest pale glow emitted from her, and though I could still see through her ghostly apparition, her beautiful features, from raven hair to piercing green eyes, were as real and vivid as they had been before we parted.

In my stupor I managed to call out to her in the faintest of tones. My Alice continued to look out for a moment before slowly turning to face me as if in some ghostly stupor of her own. Upon catching my gaze, she gave a speechless smile, loving and sincere—yet with a sympathetic sorrow that stabbed at my heart.

"Alice . . . " I began. But the sea of emotions flowing within me was too much to bear; my voice fading as if lost and drowning in the barrier between the dead and living. Wretched as I was, I picked myself up from my sitting chair, but in some cruel manner my Alice was nowhere to be found. Gone as quick as she had mysteriously appeared, the pale glow of the moon silently pouring from an empty windowsill.

The following morning I awoke to the sound of Alphonse; a series of quiet, but concerned pleas drew me back again to my cold reality. He sat there patiently waiting for me near the foot of my chair, scruffy as always. The winter sun was beginning to peek through the window, and for a moment her ghostly portrait flashed in my mind.

I croaked: "Yes, just a minute, my friend," standing up from my chair and tightening my robe, the familiar warmth of Alphonse against my legs. I slowly made my way over to the kitchen with Alphonse trailing behind and poured some milk.

"There you are." Alphonse began on his drink; and I on the remaining alcohol in my glass from the night prior, then from the bottle itself that had been sitting on the table a few moments after finishing the glass. I poured a little more milk in Alphonse's dish for good measure. "I suppose we can both drink away our sorrows." The remaining two of us sat silently together with our respective beverages.

I slowly hung my head.

The heavy sigh I produced interrupted the silence of the empty house. "Oh, Alice," almost in tears once again, "why was the world so cruel to us?" I folded my arms and moved facedown on the table. *Was there something you were trying to tell me? Did you come to stay . . . ? For our anniversary?* It couldn't have been a dream—a dream doesn't engrave like that.

Alphonse stopped drinking and gave a satisfied meow. "Had enough, I suppose."

I gave a quiet hollow laugh, "Can't say the same for me." My bottle went up. Mid-swig and half startled, I felt Alphonse once again rubbing against the bottom of my legs. I watched the scruffy, dirty orange mass of fur manoeuvre around my ankles in some sort of makeshift figure eight pattern. I reached down and gave a pet. He responded with a quiet meow.

"That's a good fellow."

Now some purring.

Alphonse had been a lot more affectionate as of late. Poor thing; my Alice had left him too, after all.

She was always so fond of Alphonse—ever since she found him caught in the brambles near the house. Just a scared, lost little kitten who'd strayed too far.

"Oh, we must keep him, Dimitri!" she said, petting the poor kitten who just almost fit in her hands. "Just look at him." She held her arms outstretched, and I was met with a pair of innocent eyes gazing back at me from a small scruffy face.

"You're scaring him, swinging him around like that."

"I am not!" she said, cradling him. "I think he quite likes it." She made a gentle, elegant spin in place before playfully sticking her tongue out in response to my exaggerated wincing. "Don't mind him, Blaze."

"Blaze? You've already given the thing a name? And a bad one at that, too."

"Yes. Yes I have," she said, her lips forming a smile. She placed the kitten down in the makeshift crate bed. "And *I* happen to think it's a great name."

I looked at my Alice, trying to put on a concerned face, but couldn't resist showing the hint of a smile—she and that cat would make a happy pair. Her warm green eyes looked back at me, loving and lit, awaiting my response.

"What am I to do with you," I sighed in a half laugh.

"So we're keeping him then, yes?"

"Yes, I suppose we can," I said. "Maybe he'll catch us a few mice."

"Oh splendid! Thank you, Dimitri, Thank you!" She jumped up and flung her arms around me, kissing me on the cheek.

"But we're not naming him Blaze. That's too generic."

"Then what would you suggest?" she said, arms around my neck.

I pondered for a short moment. "'Alphonse' is a nice name," I said. "Dignified. Nice for a cat, hm?"

"Well, I guess that'll have to do." She put her hands on my shoulders now. "Got to let you have *something* of a say in this." She went over to Alphonse's crate, his curious head popping up with pointed ears as she reached out to pet him. "But it is something of a horrid name," she laughed, turning to smile at me.

"She grew on it though, didn't she, Alphonse?" I straightened back up to reach again for my drink on the kitchen table. "Didn't she . . . ?"

Alphonse's meow seemed to echo in the empty home.

After a few moments, a storm of thoughts and emotions ran through my head. *Why did she appear?* Nothing made sense. Something was clearly wrong. My Alice was gone; I saw her lowered into the grave, flower in hand. I stayed there for hours. *What did my Alice want to tell me?*

I rose from the kitchen chair and made my way back to the piano room. Seeing the abandoned windowsill where my Alice had mysteriously appeared to me made me feel as if I were about to collapse. *Where had she gone? Why would my Alice do this?* All the dark emotions and trauma from the past few weeks began to spark again, festering and overwhelming. I slowly fell to the floor, on my knees.

"Why . . . ?" I asked, shaking now. "I want her back. I want my Alice back!" It felt too cruel. "Alice!" I shouted, "Alice!"

Silence.

The windowsill looked back at me. I needed her back. I needed to heal. "ALICE!" I tried again, my voice breaking now. "Where did you go?" I pounded my fist on the floor, over and over again. The pain was unbearable; I wanted it gone—I wanted everything gone.

I lay on the floor, broken. Alphonse meandered into the room and climbed on the windowsill to lie in the last wisps of sun, peering out at the dead brambles below.

The subsequent days all melded into one great miserable ruin. I wandered through the empty haunted halls of my once warm home, looking, searching for a sign of my Alice. Alphonse and whiskey were the only friends I had left. The days were void of any light or life, and the nights continued to feel darker and colder and barren. I thought, *just maybe*, that I might see her one more time; that I could be ready this time and withstand the pain so as to not break down at the sight of my beloved Alice.

I waited at that same spot, for hours on end, staring at an empty windowsill in torturous lament, my sighs dragging me lower and lower.

"Alice will be here," I reassured Alphonse. "She'll come back."

But after many dark, desperate hours just willing my Alice to reappear—to at least show a sign she had been here and that her ghostly image was not merely a dream—the dreadful reality that my Alice had left me once again began to sink in like a poisonous, cold, dull knife.

Sitting at the piano, playing for no one but Alphonse who was lying atop the instrument, the sad tune, painful and desolate, reverberated through the house. The crackling fire filled the room with its only light: a warm glow that brightened the room, yet failed to comfort. Outside a light snow fell on a quiet, moonlit night.

Alphonse meowed at the end of my piece.

"Liked that one, huh?" I closed the piano lid. "It's nice, isn't it?" I turned in my seat to face the lonely fire, mesmerized by its dancing flames, pondering. There was nothing I could do to fill the empty void in me; my Alice wasn't coming back. Her ghostly appearance seemed to be a fleeting image that would forever haunt, leaving me plagued with the constant desire for my lost Alice that could never return—not even as a ghost.

Clasping my hands, the wedding ring on my finger glimmered in the light of the sombre flames. I was sure my Alice had come back for our anniversary. After all, it was only a few days away now.

My insides seemed to grow heavier and darker.

Maybe she will come back, it occurred to me. *Maybe she was simply waiting.* I would just have to wait for that day, too.

But despite the sliver of comfort that the idea of an eventual reunion gave, the thought of having to wait just a few days longer only underlined the abysmal loneliness within. I looked around myself and became absorbed in the isolation of the dark lit room.

I needed my Alice now; her absence was killing me.

Alphonse suddenly fell off the piano and dropped onto my lap, seemingly unharmed.

"Be careful there . . . "

Then, a thought came across my mind: "Perhaps it's time to go once again," I said quietly, scratching the back of Alphonse's furry head. Maybe my Alice was waiting there. But it felt like it had been so long; the thought of going only to find nothing overwhelmed me with dread. But the agony of never trying and never seeing her at all was far greater.

By the late midday after another lonely night, I had finally left.

A concerned Alphonse tried to follow me outside, meowing incessantly at this odd behavior, curious as to what was so wrong that I had to leave the house.

As I stepped out, the world around me, that had once felt so full of life and happiness, never felt more dull and depraved.

Walking on the snow covered path, the forest of leafless trees all around, reminded me again of the barren and pathetic state that my life had turned into. Thin fog that covered the path curled around the tree branches like ghostly vines and seeped down the edge of the great cliff far to the side, beyond the shrubs and trees. The static gray overcast above shrouded all in a bleak darkness that drained the color and life out of everything. Sun was nowhere to be found.

A cold wind that whistled against bark and rushed between branches seemed to cut right through me. I readjusted my collar and tightened my scarf, with hair and coat blowing in the wind, yet still felt no warmth to guard or comfort. The general quiet of the lifeless forest isolated me in a void of terrible loneliness. My Alice was not too far ahead now.

The low iron fence came into view a midst the dreary fog and snow. Entering through the gateway, I walked on the brick path covered by a translucent thin sheet of white. I looked about, making my way over to my Alice while snow continued to fall. The dozens of gravestones around me, most old and wearing, oozed a deathly gloom into the atmosphere.

I sunk deeper into my coat. All these people had been taken away from someone—perhaps they could sympathize with me. However, my case was different. My Alice had been taken from me when we still had a whole life ahead of us. Stolen, leaving me with a missing half.

We were so happy . . . *Funny, how things can change so quickly.*

"Aren't they just lovely, Dimitri?" Alice said to me as I was lying under the oak tree. She motioned at all the buttercups in the grassy field in front of us, back towards me. Her raven hair, flowing out from under an elegant straw hat, gently swayed in the soft wind. I picked a buttercup from where I lay and examined it between my two fingers, drawn by its warm and vibrant yellow.

"Yes," I said simply, "they're quite beautiful." My eyes were still fixed on the small flower. Then my gaze moved from the buttercup to Alice, who was now standing in front of me and looking back with a tender smile. "Although not as beautiful as you," I added, cheekily.

"Oh, I'm *flattered*," Alice said.

"I must say, you've chosen an excellent spot for our picnic."

"Nothing but the best." She lay down next to me with her green eyes looking up at the sky through the swaying leaves, rays of sunlight shining between. "Makes you appreciate the beauty of it all—of life." She brushed her hand through the grass.

We sat together in quiet happiness under the great tree.

"Really, I could lie here forever," I said softly.

Alice gave a gentle laugh and laced her fingers with mine.

Around us, the buttercups in the green field rustled in the wind amid the sigh of the tree.

"I could die a happy man right now."

I felt my hand squeezed.

Now walking through the graveyard in the bitter cold, I blew into my hands, tightly pressing them together. Just a few steps further and I had reached my destination. A fresh gravestone among the old rested in front of me. I stood there facing the stone tablet in a dark silence, snow continuing to fall around me. There was no movement, just frozen in place, staring, brooding, yearning.

Finally a word escaped from my mouth.

"Alice?" I shifted from the gravestone and looked around. Nothing but a cold and gray, snow-filled void. Surely she must be here. I tried again.

"Alice, I'm here . . . It's Dimitri. I came to see you." Again, nothing but the howling wind. It felt as if my insides were breaking down, like the last remaining wisps of warmth in me were being snuffed out, causing my delicate, battered heart to slowly freeze over.

I clutched my scarf in front of the grave, spouting more feeble attempts to make contact with my Alice. The snow seemed to engulf me in its cold, and the wind continued to howl, drowning out my voice which grew weaker and weaker.

At last I stood there, defeated and more broken than ever before.

"There is no point in me being here anymore."

The wind muted my small voice. "Goodbye, Alice."

It was cold.

Back at home now, in an almost deathlike state, all seemed to turn to despair. I grew more numb by the minute after my attempt at the graveyard. But within the frozen remains of my heart, there was still one lingering ember. Our anniversary was tomorrow. That was when my Alice would be back. *This was why she appeared to me.* All I could do was wait in agony. It was all too clear there was nothing in my power I could do to see my Alice again. Waiting was the only option; my last small shard of hope.

I sat in a sort of senile anticipation on my chair, and I didn't make the slightest movement besides the ever so subtle rise and fall of each quiet breath. Alphonse would appear here and there, meowing or rubbing against my leg, but each noise from him seemed muted and distant, and his scruffy fur no longer held any warmth or feeling. All the while, the windowsill still lay deserted and the ghostly memory of my Alice subdued every thought. Tomorrow we would be reunited at last.

Time seemed to amalgamate together in some meaningless heap. Nonetheless, I was now aware it was just a few hours until our day—a few hours until this pain would fade away. But in the tired and frail state that I was in, I drifted off to sleep, unable to stay awake for the turn of the coming day.

When I eventually awoke it was to the meow of Alphonse, almost inaudible, lost in the space between the dead and living. There he sat, alone on the windowsill, with the last faint light from the fading moon spilling out behind him, welcoming the coming day.

I watched as the sunlight filled the empty room before eventually fading and fading into total darkness. It was all in vain.

Only then had my last light been completely extinguished. My Alice had left me again for what felt like the thousandth time, now ripping the remaining broken shards of my heart out of my chest and leaving me hollow. There was no point anymore—there was no point to anything. My Alice was gone.

Still in my chair, the realization that my Alice was truly gone began to soak in, like blood from a fatal wound slowly covering the surface of a dead body. It felt as if I were stuck in place, too weak and heavy to rise from where I sat, too cold to even bother trying. But despite the cold and the numbness that seemed to completely overwhelm me, a dark and ravenous storm of emotions frenzied in my mind, shrieking and reverberating in the hollow shell of my body, growing louder and louder, causing my being to crumble.

Sparked by the raging storm within, yet still held back by the cold, like an artificial rejuvenation of a frozen body, I managed to get up from my chair, almost collapsing onto the floor. A slightly startled Alphonse perked up from his resting spot, looking up with concerned cat eyes.

Standing in the middle of the room, I wanted to yell. I wanted to scream. I wanted to topple furniture, shatter bottles against the wall, tear off each painting and mirror and smash them on the floor. Yet my hands did not move; they felt like ice.

I violently jerked away upon the numb feeling of Alphonse against my leg, and I finally snapped. The room was suddenly filled by the sound of a harsh and grating scream with such pain and turmoil behind it that the very walls should have crumbled. I hurled my foot towards the terrified Alphonse with the intent to destroy anything and everything in sight. But with a sharp meow the scruffy Alphonse dashed away unharmed towards the kitchen. With surprising speed I grabbed the nearest glass bottle, heavy and firm in hand, and flung it towards the fleeing Alphonse, fragmenting it across the floor with a loud crash before expelling another horrible scream. I brought my hands up, covering my face and screaming mouth, my nails digging into flesh, shaking and staggering back a few steps.

Just as quickly as my screams filled the room, a deafening silence engulfed the atmosphere. I took several deep and shaky breaths, my wide eyes peering out through a lace of fingers. Unable to control myself, I stumbled out of the room and straight outside into the cold night.

This is the only way.

I struggled through the snow, tripping and falling several times, clawing through to get back up, its bitter and sharp cold completely numb in my hand. The silence of the night fought against the harrowing, colossal noise inside. Not a single snowflake fell from the sky, nor did the slightest wind move through the air—yet the storm of my anguish alone completely tore through the night's tranquility.

Again, I entered the forest of leafless trees, my mind set.

The only light was from that of the moon and stars splashing against the surrounding snow, creating a pale luminescent glow on the ground's surface. It revealed the silhouettes of the forest's gaunt trees, their weaving limbs backlit by the starry sky. My crazed stride began to drift away from the prior footprints that had been left there.

Though I took no notice of it, I began to gradually slow down, and with each step, my feet became heavier and heavier in the brutal cold. My chest heaved, inhaling the icy air and exhaling a great fog that rose into the sky.

I continued to struggle through the snow in a hysterical madness, making my way beyond the shrubs and trees. The senseless pain was unbearable. How was it possible that a man so hollow could be filled with such grief and anguish? How could this pain still overcome the numbness of a wound opened over and over? *Gone—Gone!—I want it GONE! Everything gone!* The thousands of voices screaming in my head had drowned what little reason and humanity I had left, leaving me a wretched and pitiful mess of pure sorrow and despair.

Soon enough, after the desperate and frantic trek through the merciless cold, I had reached my destination, my end. The great cliff lay before me, like a vast abyss of dark consolation. I stood a few steps from the cliffside, its enticing edge drawing me in with a weak, invisible pull. My feet shuffled through the snow, slowly inching closer.

Arms at my side, I overlooked the great emptiness of the cliff, my breath beginning to steady, the moon and stars looking down on me. The cool glow that shone from the snow tapered off the edge, eaten by the darkness. I peered over the cliff into the void of the unknown, hearing its tantalizing promise of relief. The incessant voices in my head started to calm, my fists unclenched, and my thoughts finally began to clear. At last, this pain would finally fade away. My days of misery and torment would be over; my hopeless hours of waiting in distress; my plaintive and pathetic nights of loneliness; my Alice—

. . . My Alice . . .

My Alice would see me soon.

Cupping my hands, and gazing out into the abyss, my feet were frozen. *Why . . .*

The solution to all the pain lay before me, yet I would not reach for it. *WHY?*

I began to stagger back a few steps before my knees gave away. I started to shiver.

The previously violent thought that had been raging in my mind now repeated itself again:

I cannot see my Alice . . .

A tear began to form on the side of my forlorn and weary face, followed by another, and then another. I slowly fell onto my side, the snow hugging around me, weeping in the calm silence of the night with the great cliff and its vast emptiness in front.

A graceful snow began to fall, light and soft. Their cool glow, reflected from the moon and stars, glimmered in the still night a midst my quiet sobs.

I felt a snowflake on my cheek.

Sagittae Angelorum

Drama—I

"Kintsugi"

A one-act play by Jeremy Joosten

Characters

Character X: An older person who has only ever thought about himself

Character Y: A guide to help people move on

Doctor: Doctor

Setting

A hospital room where Character X has been many times before.

Author's Notes

Like the mathematical variable, Character X is always changing. The character never likes to stay in one place, they are always looking for something to do, to go somewhere, and are never present in the moment. Throughout their long life, they have had too many accidents to count. Many accidents have happened to their head. Each accident takes them to the very same bed in the same hospital that the audience sees them in.

They had a family, and although they think that they did a good job raising their kids and treating their family, their children have distanced themselves from them. They are ignorant of this. They are very stubborn, and will only take their medicines when they must, and have a "mind over body" mentality. Up until this point in their life, their "mind over body" mentality has been a great help to them.

Like the variable, Character Y, this character is constant. Both young and old at the same time, Character Y has been around to guide characters like Character X from the world we know into a reality that is beyond ours.

They have a familiar face, the kind of face that will capture your attention if you pass by them on the street, a memorable face. This character is quiet, yet strong, humble, yet determined, and not arrogant but wise. If you had never met Character Y you would feel welcomed by them, and you would recognize them, but not recall from where you knew them.

The Doctor has seen every accident that Character X has suffered. He knows that the main character will not live long if the injuries keep happening.

Scene 1

The curtains open. There is a single bed in the center stage. An electrocardiogram, an IV drip, and other medical equipment can be seen surrounding the bed. There are no lamps, no desks, no vases, and no paintings. There is a single chair on the stage right of the bed. It is an old chair, one that has been used many times by loved ones who are saying goodbye to dear friends. In this chair sits the Doctor.

The act is to begin in darkness for 7 seconds. The beat of an electrocardiogram can be heard marking each second as it passes.

On the 7th second, a single spotlight is turned on above the bed where we can see Character X lying in a coma, not moving.

The electrocardiogram decrescendos in sound but can still be faintly heard.

The Doctor is seen with his profile to the audience, sitting on the stage right of the bed, until the 7 seconds are up. Once the spotlight turns on, the Doctor gets up and starts checking various medical instruments around Character X. The Doctor is shaking his head and talking to himself somewhat under his breath.

DOCTOR:

shaking his head with disbelief

It's a surprise he's managed to even live this long. I've never seen a patient with this extensive medical history in a coma no less.

The Doctor continues to go around checking the numerous pieces of medical equipment around Character X.

to himself

Three skull fractures in 30 years, and multiple concussions throughout his life. The list goes on and on. Every time we send him out of the hospital, he keeps finding a way to roll on back here to the same bed.

He sits back down next to Character X and pats his hand.

Only this time old timer it looks like there's little we can do to help.

The Doctor exits quietly. After the Doctor leaves, the electrocardiogram turns off. After the electrocardiogram fades to nothing, there are to be 3 seconds of silence. The overhead spotlight is still on Character X.

CHARACTER X

After the 3 seconds have passed, he starts to move his finger. He taps it on the bed a few times, then flexes his hand into a fist. He is in no pain, not stiff in any way. He opens his eyes. He sees nothing but does not immediately react to it. He does not yawn because he is not tired. Instead, he takes a deep breath in through his mouth.

angrily

Why isn't anyone here?

to himself

Maybe this time, I had a terrible accident. Did I have an accident? I can't remember if the accident was my fault. Of course, it wasn't my fault, I just lost my balance so someone else must have hit me.

Tries to look around but cannot see.

I can't see anything right now, but I know I'll come around to it eventually.

Tries to get up but cannot move anything besides his head. Character X tries again to get up but can't. He grunts, straining, to move but nothing seems to be working. It is almost as if he has become stuck to the bed.

This isn't right. I'm trying to move but I can't feel my hands or legs. I can't feel the sheets beneath them. I'm using every bit of will to move but I can't.

Calls out to the side where he thinks a nurse would be.

Hello! Can anyone hear me?! I can't move and it's starting to get annoying! Hello!! Nurses?! Ahh! I always get the lazy nurses who can't hear anything! HELLO?!?

Out of breath, Character X comes to a shocking realization.

Wait a minute. I can't hear my heart machine. Where are the little beeps? The sound of the IV drip?

Pauses to listen.

Oh God, I've become deaf too!! Can anyone hear me? I need help I can't see, I can't hear, and I'm stuck in this bed! Wait, am I even saying anything? Am I speaking if no one is around to hear my cries for help? Am I even speaking if no one cares to listen? Oh no, no, no I've become a mute too!!"

Now blind, deaf, and mute Character X starts sobbing quietly with his head down.

Defeated and almost in a whisper he calls out.

Is there anyone out there who will listen to what I have to say?

The lights slowly dim as Character Y walks on stage from stage left. As he is walking on, Character X is still quietly sobbing and does not notice Character Y, as he sits next to Character X's left foot at the corner of the bed.

CHARACTER Y

chuckling

Of course, someone's listening. Someone's always listening

Character X, still caught up in his new reality, doesn't acknowledge Character Y just yet. Character X lets out a long and rather humorous wail shaking his head as he does so.

Character Y becomes excited that Character X can move his head. He places his hand on Character X's foot and shakes it gently.

CHARACTER Y

Did you see that? You moved around all on your own! You'll be ok. Don't worry, you're not blind, you're not paralyzed to this bed, and you are not mute, that I can assure you.

Character X realizes that someone's there with him in the room. He still cannot see who it is, but he reaches for the hand that touches his leg. He sits up in the bed, following the arm of Character Y up to the shoulder. He pauses, thinking.

CHARACTER X

You don't seem to be any nurse that I know. What kind of nurse sits on the patient's bed? Pff, all the nurses I know barely even stop by my room. Have you heard how long I've been calling for help?

CHARACTER Y

Would I be wrong in saying that you're the kind of person who never asks for help? It must've been really important if you were asking for help just now.

CHARACTER X

Now able to see, can look Character Y in the face. Character X can now move his hands, but not his feet.

Oh, now I see you. No, I never ask for help. And what's the point? I know that if I ask someone else to help me two things can happen. One: No one listens because they are too busy with their own issues. You ask, and you ask, calling out to everyone for help. But no one ever listens. Everyone's life is too busy. Everyone has their problems to deal with, and why would I want them to neglect their own mess to clean up mine? I would have to be the most selfish person in the world to ask for someone else's help. And two: No one cares about other people's problems. They blame others for the mistakes that they've made. Blaming someone's poverty on a lack of work ethic or someone's addiction is the result of a bad upbringing. It was *their own* choice to mess up their life. If I help them then they might mess up my life too.

No, there's no point in asking other people for help. People can't even help themselves.

Pauses and points at himself.

Look at me.

You were the first person to ever listen to me. Why are you even here?

CHARACTER Y

I am here to help you.

Stands up and gently pulls off the covers of the bed. He pulls Character X into a sitting position and removes the IV from Character X's arm.

Where you are now, will take some getting used to. If you want to leave this hospital and never need to come back here, you will have to accept my help.

Pulls Character X's legs off the side of the bed. Character X is now sitting with his legs off the bed and can freely move his two feet, but not his legs. Character X flexes his feet.

CHARACTER Y

sternly

You will need to understand that there have been people, loved ones, friends, and strangers, who have helped you in the past. People who have cared about you, your goals, and your well-being even when you have not noticed it. You have hurt them. Especially your loved ones. You have neglected them due to your stubborn mentality. You have hurt them, with your own self-centered decisions.

CHARACTER X

Looks confused. He cannot remember what he did to his loved ones that would have caused these accusations. Character Y, noticing the confusion on Character X's face, eases up on his friend.

CHARACTER Y

This is going to be hard to understand at first. Your lifetime of head injuries has caused your brain to work differently than most. Your concussions and fractures have rewired your brain and psyche to become the individualistic person you are today.

Steps back, about 6 feet away from the bed. He folds his arms, almost challenging Character X to get up and come to him.

You asked why I am here. I am here to help you move on to the next part of your life. To guide you. I am to help you see, feel, and hear the moments in your life when your own blindness, deafness, and lack of speech have caused you to fracture your closest relationships. And it is going to start with you standing up, out of that bed.

CHARACTER X

Looks down at his legs.

But I can't even feel my legs. They cannot move. No matter how hard I try, I'm not even able to place one foot in front of the other.

Starting to get frustrated and angry. Slapping his legs, moving them around, trying to get any feeling into the legs.

My legs have become dead and stiff. I have forgotten what it is like to wiggle my toes, feel the air on my skin, the grass underneath my feet. All this gone, and you still want me to move?!

CHARACTER Y

That's right.

CHARACTER X

Let's out a puff of disbelief.

That's not possible.

CHARACTER Y

How is it not possible? Think about how far you have come to reach this point. Minutes ago, you were barely able to move. You couldn't see or move your hands, now you're sitting here slapping your legs!

I know you. I've known you your whole life. You pushed through every challenge that has come your way. War, fractures, comas, concussions, and brain trauma, all came and went. It has hardened you. Your relationship with your wife was more difficult because of all your injuries. Your interactions with your children have been skewed because of your brain trauma. What you saw as a gift was a burden to them. The training, the hikes, and the trips that you took them on, while enjoyable to you, created a rift between you and your children.

You sit here and complain about not being able to walk.

On your daughter's last day of kindergarten, you rewarded her by taking her on a 40-mile two-day hike. This was the beginning of many grueling hiking trips that you took her on. You loved it, the fresh air, the wind, the grass beneath your feet.

But did you stop to think about what *she* felt on that hike? What has it felt like to walk for an eternity in the eyes of a child? How that could have changed the relationship that you two had? Do you remember what you said to your daughter as she complained about her feet feeling dead and stiff?

You stopped to turn around and look at her. What did you see?

Acting out the part of the daughter.

Your daughter, a little girl, exhausted, standing with her arms folded with a stubborn glance on her face. Waddling side to side on the trail with a big backpack on her and a grumpy look on her face. She didn't know you were watching because she was just staring at her feet. She didn't know how long the journey was but kept trudging on, tired and grumpy. Although you could not express it on your face, you were so proud of the little girl you saw before you. How she had walked all this way just to be with her father. Then she looked up and saw you. With childlike drama, she fell to the ground and said she did not want to get up and was going to live there, on the trail, for the rest of her life.

"What about home?" you asked her. "If you stay here on the trail, you're never going to make it back home and see your brothers and mom again. That means we would have to throw out all of your toys." Boy, did that get her up and off the ground quickly.

The lesson that she learned that day is the same lesson that you are to learn. Yes, you are exhausted and do not want to move. But it is possible to move on. You've lived a long life and are not sure of what comes next. But you must keep progressing. Put one foot in front of the other, and waddle along like a kindergartner on the trail that will take you back to your family. You cannot stay here if you want to see them.

CHARACTER X

Moved by the detail of the story. It was his story.

I almost forgot about that day. I wanted to give her a present that she'll never forget. But it was a present that *I* wanted, not what *she* wanted. What kindergartener would want to go on a 40-mile hike? Ahh, I should not have done that. I should have taken the time to think about what she thought about the hike. I always did whatever *I* wanted to do. I guess I assumed my kids liked to do what I like instead of them liking something else. I wish I could go back and fix it.

Looking over to Character Y.

Am I able to fix our relationship?

CHARACTER Y

Life is a strange thing. A person spends their life torn between three places: today, tomorrow, and yesterday. They think today about what should have been done yesterday, and rarely think about what will happen tomorrow. Caught in an infinite loop of regret and neglect, they are never able to exist in the present. Once today is gone and tomorrow is here, a person recognizes the mistakes they made yesterday. They wish they could fix it, that little mistake in the past, and keep glancing back at it wishing it didn't happen.

No. You are not able to fix your relationship with your daughter. Come take a step."

CHARACTER X

Realizes that Character Y's right.

You're right. I'm no longer able to turn around on this trail and fix where I came from. If I want to continue toward home, I must keep moving.

Slowly lowers himself off the bed. His legs cannot stand the weight of his feet at first. His legs sink with the weight of his body, and he ends up kneeling on the ground. He cannot move or look up. Character Y quietly walks over and grabs his hands. He pulls Character X effortlessly off the ground. Character X puts his arms out to check his balance and can now stand there firmly. He takes a timid step forward. Pauses, as he is out of breath from this one step.

CHARACTER Y

You will find that you have a hard time moving on. You are too attached to your belongings to continue to move on. You will have to let them go.

CHARACTER X

What belongings? Where? I am standing here in nothing but my revealing hospital gown. How can I have any belongings left with me!?

CHARACTER Y

I am not talking about belongings that you physically carry with you, but belongings that you carry with you close to your heart. The physical and emotional attachments from your life weigh you down has made it difficult for you to walk.

CHARACTER X

grumbling

Seems like you're doing a lot more talking and judging than helping me learn to walk.

CHARACTER Y

Remember, I am here to help you *learn* to walk down your path again, not to carry you the whole way. Yes, it is my job to walk *with* you, not for you. And to get you to walk again, I will need to continue to share with you how your past continues to affect you in the present.

You've never backed down from a challenge, despite how unlikely it is you'll win. You care about keeping what you love safe. It didn't matter if it was one of your children or one of your belongings, you will fight for what is yours and never let anyone take it from you. Do you recall the time that the guy tried to rob your car?

It was during the night. You had come back from work, barely even legal at 21 years old, and decided to go stop by a bar with some co-workers.

It was a great night. You had a car that you just bought, and new work friends to bond over drinks with. For the first time since immigrating to this country, you felt like you were welcomed. You laughed with your new friends, raising a toast to each other, singing bar tunes till the early morning. It felt like home.

The night soon came to an end, and you went back out to your car. You saw your friend, your closest coworker, and it looked like he was trying to break into your car. Angry and offended that he would even think about touching your car, you yelled at him and punched him away from the car. He fell back and yelled back something in English. You had no idea what he was saying, English was hard enough to listen to by itself, and the sound of it only worsened with alcohol. You yelled back at him, and he pulled out a knife. With a quick thrust, his knife came inches from your neck. But you managed to block it, with the back of your hand, saving both your life and your car.

You needed 27 stitches in your left hand. The tendons attached to your middle, ring, and pinky fingers had been severed, and although they were somewhat successfully reattached, they never worked the way they used to. It took four months of therapy for you to regain function in your hand. You also changed jobs and lost the friends you were with that night.

CHARACTER X

Looks down at his hand and flexes it, remembering the story.

I remember what happened. I never understood how someone could be so *stupid* as to try to break into a car right in front of its owner.

CHARACTER Y

Look more closely. Maybe he thought he was the car's owner? Or more accurately, after having one too many drinks, maybe he thought that it was *his* car. Maybe he wasn't trying to break into a stranger's car and steal what doesn't belong to him, but simply trying to get back into his car and head home. He was scared when he saw a foreign man shove him, and yell at him in a language he did not know. He tried to yell back, to use his words and explain the misunderstanding, but it got nowhere. Backed into a corner and drunk from the bar, he felt like he had no choice but to lash out in anger.

Pointing to Character X.

You were too attached to your possessions.

You saw your best friend trying to take your car and reacted in anger. You punched him. You escalated the situation from one of simple misinterpretation into one of danger and harm. As a result, you lost the function of your left hand.

Was it worth it?

Was your car worth the friends that you lost that night? The job you loved, the people you celebrated with, that feeling of home, gone. Just because you valued your car and its safety over your own. If you hadn't been lucky enough to block the knife, would you be *standing* here right now?"

CHARACTER X

No.

CHARACTER Y

Then *walk*, don't just stand. Stop looking beside you and gazing at what you have. *Look forward* to where you're going, and whom you are headed to. You have been broken, and shattered, too many times to count, but that does not matter. Like pottery that has smashed into a thousand tiny pieces, and put back together with gold, I am here to help you present your best self on the last part of your journey.

CHARACTER X

What if I'm not ready yet? My past journey, my life, has been all I've known. What comes next? Is it life again or nothing? Help me, I'm ashamed of myself.

Overcome with emotion, Character X starts to cry. Slowly. Like an old married man who realized he lost his wife, he doesn't understand the emotion that he is feeling at first. He starts to sob quietly. This is because he has realized how his relationship with others has been affected by his own decisions. Character X's physical and psychological limitations led him to treat others like this.

Ashamed of what I've done. Ashamed of what I didn't do. Ashamed I didn't ask for help earlier. I'm sorry.

Looks back to stage left, as if he can see his daughter, his friend, his past self.

I'm so, so sorry.

CHARACTER Y

Pauses, aware and proud of how far Character X has come to reach this point of asking for forgiveness. He takes a small step towards Character X, arms opened for a subtle embrace.

My friend, you don't need to be ashamed. You weren't meant to have this level of insight into your life until you reached this part of your journey. You're forgiven. Not by me, but by your daughter. Although it took her decades to understand your point of view, she came to understand that you didn't take her on those hikes to punish her. She realized that you were sharing your passions with her. She gradually learned to love it. She loved it so much that she still goes mountain climbing today, as a mountain rescue team member. She's saved so many lives on the same mountains you love. Because you decided to bring that little kindergartener on a hike and tell her to keep going. To never give up and keep walking home.

Spread his arms bigger. Reaching out with outstretched hands, it almost looks like he is in the shape of a cross.

Now it's your turn. Don't give up. Walk to me, walk home, towards the new part of your life.

CHARACTER X

Takes one second to pause. Then, without any struggle, walks into the outstretched arms of Character Y. They embrace. The lights dim, and as the lights are dimming, the two walk off stage left.

Fin

Sagittae Angelorum

Short Stories—III

by Jeremy Joosten

The Artist, the Statue, & the Fox

Before buildings became more common than trees, back when we looked toward the stars for navigation, there was a very creative being who was known only as the Artist. Legend had it that he was banished from his home tribe long ago. Nobody knew why, but everyone acknowledged the fact that this backstory likely inspired his creations. The Artist walked to every corner of the earth, creating something new in each location. Each was a greater masterpiece than the last, standing proud for centuries.

But there is one creation that is less known. A sculpture that was created from the very core of the Artist's emotions and feelings.

This is the story about the Statue & the Fox.

After he was banished from his tribe, the Artist found himself in the middle of the world. It was silent. Nothing had lived there before. Having been banished from his tribe, the Artist felt like he could never live again. He tore his hands through the earth. Weeping and letting out a cry that had never been heard before, the Artist created clay from nothing but the dust and his tears. He pushed the clay together, putting all his pain into the creation.

He did not stop making the statue until he ran out of tears. Gasping, weak from his tears, he stopped. He stood up with his eyes closed, laid his hand on the heart of the Statue and paused. Then he turned around and left without looking back. Time moved on slowly, and the Artist died. Alone and by himself, with no one to care for him.

Staring ahead, hoping for the return of its creator, the Statue still sat there. It sat hoping, for someone, something, to come to visit.

No one came.

Snow fell, and leaves blossomed, but still, the Statue remained the same. Trapped and dreaming about being able to run free and see what's beyond its line of vision. Sweet dreams that gave it hope. Still, the Statue hated being trapped. The Statue was so frustrated at times that, if someone was present, they could have seen the tears streaming from its face on rainy days.

The Statue learned, in time, to notice the small improvements in its surroundings. The trees were growing with alarming speed around it. The Statue noticed that the trees had eventually turned into a forest. The sun even seemed to be brighter than it was in the past. But the most important addition to its surroundings was the Fox.

Some time ago, she had chosen the Statue as a home. Every day the Fox would wake up and say hello to the Statue, rub her fur against its base, then slowly jog off into the woods. And every evening she would return and lay at the foot of the Statue, sighing and barking as if she was telling the Statue about her day. The Fox seemed to know that there was a good quality about the Statue, that it was there to listen and provide for her.

Never had the Statue felt like it was needed, like it was loved. The Statue liked that it could provide shelter and protection for something it cared for. With every season, the Statue loved the Fox more.

In an early spring month, the Fox crept out from her den underneath the Statue and said hello like she usually did. She stopped before she ran off into the woods and looked back at the Statue as if to say goodbye.

Very little time had passed before the loud sound of voices could be heard. There were gunshots and growls from dozens of dogs. A snap of a trap, and the cry so close to the Statue's heart that it made the Statue shake. The Statue wanted to help, to move the Fox out of harm's way, but it couldn't.

Limping with urgency the Fox came back to the Statue. With a small cry, she looked up at the Statue that she knew as her home. The Fox made it back, she was safe! So she thought, as the Fox took a breath to lie down and rest in front of her Statue.

Silence.

The Statue looked down at the Fox that it loved for so long. Shuddering, the Statue began to cry, with a passion that had not been seen for generations since the creation of the Statue itself. The Statue let out a cry so long and loud that morning turned into night. The Statue tried to move, to get close to her, and be near her one last time, till finally, the earth shook, and the Statue tumbled down from its pedestal to finally lay with the Fox.

—

The hunters never found the Fox. After tracking the marks, they only found a pile of rubble. No one would have known that underneath the rubble was the Statue, which finally got to lay at rest with the Fox that it loved.

Lunch Thieves

I've seen them everywhere.

Back home, they were a greyish-brown color. They were friendly. Polite even.

Heck, I even had one as a pet that I named Cinnamon. May he rest in peace.

Here, they are different. Meaner, darker, more ruthless and mischievous. They don't turn away when you look at them, no, they stare back at you, into your soul. Begging you for a challenge.

And challenge them I did.

It happened on a Sunday. I was sitting outside of the Church, after Mass, when I saw a picnic table right across the clearing. I stopped by my car and took out my lunch.

It was a very nice lunch; a simple cheese and meat sandwich with chips smashed in the middle, a small grape juice box, and a bag of carrots. I was looking forward to eating my meal. I sat through the whole service, positively dreaming about this sandwich. I know my mind should've been elsewhere, but my growling stomach just couldn't help it.

I sat down on the bench and took out my lunch. Beautiful, delicious, just what I needed after that really long homily (it always feels like a long homily). But just before I took a bite, they came.

One by one. Skittering over the leaves, jumping off the trees, pouncing on my table. They climbed up to the picnic spot, on top of the table, and stood there. Not three feet from my face, they looked at me.

They wanted my food.

"No, you stupid squirrels I don't want to give you my food! I've been waiting for this all day, and I don't want to give you any! Haven't you got enough food stored away for winter that you could find somewhere else? Why are you black and not grey or red anyways, that makes no evolutionary sense."

And they stared at me. Their eyes were as black and cold as their skin. They crept slowly inching forward, not cautious of me at all. Tiny step by tiny step they kept approaching me. It was as if they weren't scared of me at all. Unnerved, I didn't move. I wasn't sure what they would do so I just remained still.

The leader came up to my face and we were almost eye to eye. I saw a distorted, black version of myself in his lifeless eyes. A reflection of a different, but similar, person.

"That can't be me," I said out loud. "I don't look that weird."

And the squirrel punched me in the face.

I don't remember what happened after that. I only know that I woke up, on the grass, underneath the picnic table next to the Church. My face hurt and I could tell that my eye was swollen shut. I tried looking for the squirrels but never found them. My wallet was gone, my car keys, and my cell phone. All gone.

But the most awful crime they committed was taking my lunch from me before I could eat it.

Knights & Horses

I once knew a boy.

He was a young boy, barely old enough to wonder what was for dinner that night, a boy who loved his imagination and let his mind tell what he wanted to see, not what he saw.

He loved his dog. Every day, he would take his dog outside and play with him in the grass for hours on end. No longer a boy or a dog, the two were a knight and his noble steed. Together they would charge into battle, for the Glory of God and People, to defeat the enemy and win the heart of the princess.

They were inseparable.

But his dog didn't like the boy very much. The dog only hung out with the boy because there was nothing else to do.

But how could the boy know that?

Over time, they continued to grow older and more mature. The boy still loved his dog even though they no longer played in the grass like they used to. Every time the boy saw the dog, he felt like he was a kid again. He felt once again like a knight admiring his trusty steed, and his love for his dog was constantly rekindled.

Eventually, the boy moved away.

He rarely thought about his dog, he was far too busy with other things. He focused on his career and making long-lasting relationships, trying his best to set up a life that would be good for him. I know that the boy missed his days of knighthood but was afraid to admit it.

On a quiet night in the middle of the week, he got a phone call from his Mother. "You need to come back. There's nothing else we can do for him".

The boy's heart was torn.

His past and his childhood were at an end. The boy was too far away to do anything about it; there wasn't time for him to fly back to see his dog. He was distraught, crying about a childhood that had gone by too fast.

The boy never forgot about his dog.

I know, and you know, that the dog didn't really care about the boy. And yet, he still played with him.

A knight, without his horse, is a man that is an immovable object, an object shelled away from the world. A horse, without his knight, is just a rapid and untamed fury of emotions. Battles cannot be won with one and not the other. For the Glory of God and People, the man and the beast must work together.

A Story about Rain

Like most days, it was dark, grey, and wet. Like the Prairies that I was so familiar with, the rain seemed never-ending. It weighed on me. With each drop it pressed into me, applying more and more pressure to a life that was already tense.

More than anything else, I felt like complaining. Why me? What did I do? What caused this to happen to me? I wanted to swing out at the universe, and punch back at all the raindrops constantly hitting me. But I would never, could never, win. No matter what I did, the rain would always have the last hit.

Walking back from work, during a terrible storm, I noticed that the puddles were larger than they usually were. What used to be half a dozen puddles were now two pools of water bigger than a square block.

Hmm. That's not good.

I've too much to worry about right now, this puddle won't bother me.

I kept walking.

The next day, I saw the two pools had merged on the way home. What used to be a large puddle was now the size of a lake.

That's starting to be a problem. I can still work with it. There's other stuff to worry about anyways.

When I woke up in the morning, I did the usual early morning requirements to get ready. I took a shower, combed my hair, had my coffee, made my breakfast, brushed my teeth, went to the bathroom, and put on my clothes. I went to grab the keys from my dresser and walked out the front door.

That's not the view I'm used to.

As far as my eyes could see, was still flat water. No trees, no plants, no animals, no houses. Just flat water, it looked like a mirror. I could see the bright blue sky reflected on the water, giant Cumulus clouds drifting along the surface, and a few birds flying along the water.

I knelt on the porch to see how deep the water was. I stuck my hand in, expecting no more than an elbow length of puddle water. Instead, I fell headfirst into the water. I felt no bottom.

Struggling to get up, I swam to the surface and heaved myself out of the water. I lay there, starting to warm up by the sun.

Did I make this happen? Is this my fault? Could I have avoided this? I asked aloud to myself.

There was no response, only the faint sound of the birds' wings flapping over the water.

The sun slowly set, and I watched as the last rays of sunlight left.

It could be worse. At least it wasn't raining.

The Tree Boat

I had been sitting in the middle of the ocean for quite some time. Reflecting on my decisions, it might not have been the best idea to try and surf down the coast on top of a dead tree.

But hey, live and learn.

I got used to spending time there out in the ocean, I was able to crawl into one of the holes in the truck and used it as a space to sleep. I'd grown up fishing, so I wasn't worried about food. What concerned me was the fish.

What I caught wasn't anything like I had seen before. They were a wide variety of sizes and shapes. Like most fish, they were weird looking. But even worse than their looks, all the fish seemed to be conscious.

It was like they all had thoughts, feelings, and knowledge beyond their years. Every time I dangled my bait in front of them, they swam up to it, looked at it, and then right at me. They sat there, moving their fins around loosely, staring into me. The creepy thing about fish is that they don't look like they breathe. They looked like hollowed-out souls, floating in the depths of the blue infinity, waiting to be pulled up and out to the light.

They wanted to be caught.

That bothered me. I don't remember how far I was in my journey aboard the Tree Boat when I started to talk to the fish. Speaking to them as if they understood me.

"There there, buddy it's OK. Come here! I know you want to swim over here with me." And after I would talk to them, the fish would go right up and bite the bait.

When I ran out of rope, I tried to see if I could catch them by hand. I dipped my arms out in the water. Immediately, a fish the size of my palms swam directly into my cupped hands. He sat there, snuggled against my fingers, looking into my eyes. Go ahead, it's okay, he seemed to be telling me.

I cried that night when I ate him.

"It's not fair! Why me and not him?!" I yelled, tearing apart my Tree Boat. "What does he have that's worth giving that I can't give!" I ripped off the branches, pulled apart the roots, and threw everything into the ocean. I smashed my fists repeatedly into the trunk. I cried out, wishing anyone would hear me, for someone to know that I am here somewhere in the ocean.

Hours later, when I lost my voice and my eyes hurt from the salt, I stood at the tip of my Tree Boat. It was nighttime, and the stars were reflected into the water, and I couldn't tell which way was up and which way was down. I felt like I was standing directly between two worlds.

I looked down at my reflection. Coming up from the depths of the ocean was the most beautiful and majestic fish I had ever seen. His skin glistened like the color of the northern lights. He approached just below the surface, not yet ready to breach the water. When I looked into his eyes, I felt at peace. I knew that I could survive off this beautiful creature for the rest of my life.

But I couldn't do it.

Instead of asking him to sacrifice himself for me, I spread my arms wide, took a breath, and joined him in the other world.

The Journey of a Goldfish

I had a good life while it lasted. My house looked more like a castle than it did a house, and I had a wonderful view from outside my window. I used to go around in circles in my little yard, thinking and moving about, wondering what could be beyond my window. I had plenty of food, and the weather and temperature were always nice.

Every day I'd watch as if through a glass wall, as the person who gave me food walked in and poured my dinner from the ceiling. I would always watch, fascinated, as the food came streaming down from the heavens. It was like a miracle. Not ever wanting to waste that miracle, I never allowed more than a second to be wasted before I quickly went around and ate all the food that I could.

Nighttime would come and I'd get so very lonely. This is when I would stare looking out my window into what is beyond. Looking down from the window where I was staying, I saw a tree. In the tree was a large treehouse, strong, with a red roof and sides made of oak. There was a zipline that connected the house to the treehouse. I would frequently see the person who gave me food ride it into that treehouse. I wanted to try to get there myself, to leave my little bubble and see what is beyond.

For the first time in my life, I looked up and moved to the surface where the food would pour down from. Glancing down to see my little castle, I felt like a giant.

Woah, I'm really doing this.

I pushed beyond, jumped out from the surface, and landed in a heap right next to the window. The space surrounding me felt drier than what I was used to, there was air blowing onto me from every surface.

This was a mistake! I thought. But I can't give up yet, I need to make it to the treehouse.

I got up and struggled towards the window. I flopped my way up and sat on the brink of the windowsill. Right before I grabbed onto the zipline handle, I looked back at the home where I grew up. My castle, the only thing I've ever known, the place where I had all my memories. I glanced at my person who used to feed me.

So long and thank you.

I don't remember what happened after that. All I know is that I felt complete. Like I had achieved what I was meant to do. The only thing I remember was feeling flushed with emotions and at peace.

Sagittae Angelorum

Drama—II

Verso l'Alto

A One-Act Play by Lucas Smith

Cast of Characters:

Mr. Skeptic: an avid critic of all things

Mr. Seebelieve: an armchair materialist

Luciana: sister of Pier Giorgio

Pier Giorgio: man of the Beatitudes

Scene:

Pollone Italy, Via Pier Giorgio Frassati

Skeptic and Seebelieve are stopped outside a B&B; they are engaged in conversation.

MR. SKEPTIC

Who do you think he was?

Points at the street sign. Via Pier Giorgio Frassati.

MR. SEEBELIEVE

shrugging

Probably some local Papist, this country runs rampant with folklore and Catholic here-say.

MR. SKEPTIC

Perhaps you are quite right good friend, but still, he must have been quite the person at that, I have seen his name plastered like wallpaper around this town, Frassati this, Frassati that . . .

MR. SEEBELIEVE

Most-likely just some 12th century backwards monk, these parts were crawling with the type; corrupt, wannabe saviors, all excellent politicians. *They laugh.*

Luciana, an old lady, walks near them.

LUCIANA

Buongiorno.

MR. SEEBELIEVE & MR. SKEPTIC

Good morning madame.

MR. SKEPTIC

May I ask, my dear woman, who was this Frassati fellow who's name we cannot escape in this town?

He gestures to the street sign as reference.

LUCIANA

Looks at the street sign, smiles, then turns to the two men.

Ah yes, Pier Giorgio, not a day passes when I do not remember the warmth that came from his smile. He is now a fine jewel that reminds us of what we are all called to emulate.

MR. SEEBELIEVE

Was he a Pap—

catching himself, searching for words

Catholic?

LUCIANA

warmly

Your comment is not unheard of today, but to answer it properly, I should like to tell some of the stories that accompany this man of the Church, a young soul who loved Christ. Will you indulge me?

MR. SKEPTIC

We have nowhere to be for some time, so please, continue.

LUCIANA

Where to begin . . .

Skeptic grabs a nearby chair and provides it to the lady as she is quite old, nearing her late 90's.

Grazie.

She sits.

Oh yes, of course.

The lights dim over their half of the stage, lights rise on Pier Giorgio standing with hiking gear equipped and a pipe in his mouth, he has just hit the summit and has a confident smile with hands grasping his walking stick in front of him.

LUCIANA

Pier Giorgio was in love with the mountains, but this passion was fueled by his love of Christ. He always assured he would not miss a day of obligation; Mass had to be available.

Lights dim on Pier Giorgio and rise on the three.

MR. SEEBELIEVE

Ah, so not a monk, but what does a young mountain climber have to do with any of this? I though all this religious stuff took place in chapels and monasteries!

MR. SKEPTIC

Yes, this all sounds very nice, but I could go climb myself a good o'l mountain and none would give two thoughts to name a road after me.

Gestures towards the sign.

There must be more to this fellow yet.

LUCIANA

smiling tenderly

Yes, my dear sirs, I see my story has struck something deep, so I shall continue with out delay. Mountains are often the places where some of the greatest of saints journey to sit with God, one can but read the scriptures or the myriad of tales the Church has collected on the lives of such godly Christians to see: Sinai, Carmel, Mt. of Olives, Tabor, why not Grivola as well?

MR. SEEBELIEVE

crossing his arms

A point to you, but alas, these spiritual folk are all but practical, our time is rife with much strife, and yet he is remembered for these mere pleasurable past times.

shaking his head, dismissively

The logic eludes me.

LUCIANA

One rarely climbs a mountain for anything other than a spiritual encounter, there is nothing practical about it. I grant you that, but I would say that impracticality does not equal perhaps meaningless.

Looking away from the two men.

There is more to Pier Giorgio still however, as he was very much an Italian at heart, so love for his country was present as well.

As Luciana speaks, the light fades on her, and then a light rises on Pier Giorgio who is holding a FUCI (Federazione Universitaria Cattolica Italiana) flag.

LUCIANA

This country has been through much but has always been rooted in its culture. Mussolini attempted to unite this nation through human strength, but Pier Giorgio sought something more humble, more beautiful; something true.

Lights dim on Pier Giorgio, rise on the three.

MR. SEEBELIEVE

Looking at his feet, sighing.

And I suppose the only source for such a thing would be his dear friends in the Vatican, the setting sun of a bygone time full of bygone ideas and opinions. I don't see how Papism would be any better than Fascism when both assume themselves to be the only answer to the problems of this age.

LUCIANA

with a tender look

When men look within and find only themselves, problems arise. When one looks within to find Christ, the greatest joy ensues; that is the difference between the two, one leads themself, the other longs to be led by their head, a bride in waiting.

Lights dim on the three, rise on Pier Giorgio.

Three Italian Royal Guards wrestle the flag from Pier Giorgio and tear it in half, throwing it to the ground and exit the stage. Pier Giorgio kneels and holds both halves in his hands looking up in prayer.

MR. SKEPTIC

I thought that Christians were to be detached from this world? Why would this young man become so invested in politics and be distraught at the ripping of a flag?

Lights dim on Pier Giorgio, rise on the three.

LUCIANA

Learning to be in the world but not of it is a lesson most take a lifetime to understand, but dear Pier Giorgio saw clearly where his eternal nationality lay, a realization which freed his heart to love those in this world fiercely.

MR. SEEBELIEVE

arrogantly

I bet that I have done more still than this young chap; all he has done is climb, march, and kneel. What has he changed? A few feelings in low minded countrymen? I have done much more notable things than that humbug. I have helped grow the economy, developed land for good businesses and housing, all at good pricing I may say. I have done more than my fair share, what does he have to show? [*with a laugh*] When do I get to be acknowledged by your Pope for my service?

LUCIANA

You are an extremely gifted and blessed man.

She takes his hand and holds it tightly in gratitude, Seebelieve is surprised.

Thank you for helping so many people with the great gifts you have been given. Pier Giorgio understood even more than I do the depths of giving that we are capable of.

Lights dim, rise on Pier Giorgio.

Pier Giorgio stands in his bare feet, holding out his shoes and jacket to a man sitting on the ground in tattered dirty clothes.

LUCIANA

He never told anyone of his time spent among the people, the Italians whom God loved so tenderly but we forget too easily. There Pier Giorgio was, giving all he could. Like you sir, he had much to give from his position in society, but he was never content with having given his fair share; no, he gave till his last breath.

Lights rise on the three, dim on Pier Giorgio.

MR. SKEPTIC

How old was this young man when he died? If all you say is true, which I am struggling to digest I may add, he sounds as if he were a wise man who had witnessed many generations.

LUCIANA You are quite right, sir, in seeing his wisdom as extraordinary, he saw the world with an ancient light that very few come to see by. His passing exposed to us all to the depths of his missionary work in Turin.

Lights dim on three, brighten on Pier Giorgio. Luciana moves to the other side holding Pier Giorgio on the ground.

LUCIANA

He was 24 when he passed away. His parents were shocked when hundreds of the poor from the city came to the funeral to honor the young man who had brought Christ to them through his kindness, gentleness, meekness, and courage.

The lights dim on Pier Giorgio, brighten on the three.

Luciana returns to her chair.

MR. SEEBELIEVE

irritated and embarrassed

So, so what? I have to die young to be a saint? My good lady, I am afraid you and I have missed the train on this one. Ha! He sounds like a nice lad, I'll give him that, but his heroics were all in vain: the poor are still here, corruption abounds, and death still comes. I'm sorry but I must leave.

Seebelieve nods goodbye and walks off stage down the center aisle.

Skeptic watches his friend leave, then turns back to Luciana.

MR. SKEPTIC

You are very knowledgeable on this gentleman; how do you know him so well? Were you one of the poor he helped?

LUCIANA

In a way, yes. I was poor, and he helped me see things in a clear light. But I was gifted with the life of being the sister to such a brother. I am humbled constantly by this fact. I have done many things in my life, but all of it seems shallow when put next to the service of my brother. I hope to honor his life through telling his story, through having people see the power of Christ working in the world in his most humble servants.

Sagittae Angelorum

Short Stories—IV

Ode to Joy:
Historical Fiction

by Joelle Joosten

September 1777

Mein geschatzter enkel, Louis, *My prized grandson, Louis,*

You must become the finest musician in all of Europe. I invested in your father all his life, but his stale voice and drunken behavior tarnished our Beethoven name. Johann lacks the energy and passion for music that I see in you. Alas, something good has come from your father's marriage. You are my pride and joy. You will make something of yourself, thanks to my help.

This journal is a gift for you to mark the successes throughout your life. It begins now, my dear boy. I arranged for you to perform for the court in Cologne as a child protege. Mozart will be the guest of honor. Get his approval, mark my words! You mustn't let me down, for your future depends on it. If your performance is a success, the world will open to you, and Music itself may be indebted to the great name Ludwig van Beethoven. Practice well, my boy! Six hours a day. Do not forget.

dein tapferer Held, *your valiant Hero,*
Kapellmeister Ludwig van Beethoven.

P.S. I included a portrait of myself in this package for you to remember me. Send my kind regards to Mozart.

October 1777

Dear Diary,

Wow! My very own journal! I love to write. Calligraphy, stories, notes, and—oh yes! music—I love writing music! I can only write counterpoint right now. Maybe one day I can write a whole symphony! Or an opera grand enough for a real-life hero! I think music theory is too rigid, but grandfather said I must learn the rules before I can do my own thing. He also said I might have a teacher greater than him one day. I can't imagine anyone greater than my grandfather!

—Louis

April 1778

Dear Diary,

I just finished my first performance in Cologne. The one where Mozart was the guest musician! He said I am very promising, but the way I play piano is too German and choppy. Mozart seemed to forget my existence after this brief acknowledgement. I think he was also too focused on showing off, so that explains it. I'm disappointed. I thought he was a man of good taste. Seeing I played *his* music, I expected more praise for my talent.

I performed "Concerto No. 2, Opus 19," which no other eight-year-old in the world can accomplish. I think Mozart was jealous and missed being the child-protegé of Europe long ago. Oh well, at least the Duke of Bavaria thought better of me. To him, I surpassed Mozart. He praised me endlessly after the concert and gave me a gold coin.

I will mark this as a success! One down, and one lifetime of success to go!

—Louis

April 1790

"Dear Diary,"

Ha! What a cute childish title. I nearly forgot about your existence. I will come up with a new title when the inspiration finds me. Grandfather died shortly after he gave you to me. I still mourn his death, though I've lived nearly a decade in his absence. I carry his portrait with me through my various performances across Europe. How clever of grandfather to have me mark my successes, for I have many to catch you up on:

To name a few life accomplishments, I mastered the violin and viola from lessons with Franz Rovantini. I also mastered the organ with Willibald Koch O.F.M. All this before the age of 10. By the age of 12, I already understood how themes work in music. I composed a march with a theme that had nine different variations. The places a composer can go with a simple theme of three notes, or three measures is limitless!

I will never forget my first in-house teacher, Herr Tobias Pfeiffer, hired by my mother. The man received free accommodations to wake me up before dawn and remind me to practice. Every morning, the audacity! I simply couldn't stand him. Supper was no escape either, as he would recline at table with us. He said I needed to learn discipline, or my talent would go to waste. What that man didn't understand is that I had enough incentive to practice on my own accord—just not early in the morning when someone else is telling me to.

When I surpassed his skill-level, I moved up to Christian Neefe. He taught me how to compose operas. I am more inclined towards symphonies, as I believe that music speaks for itself without scripts. Opera composers use vocal text as a crutch, though they are unaware; I on the other hand, will devote my life to music in its purest form. If I ever do write an opera, it will be a beacon for future composers. Nevertheless, I learned as much from Neefe as I could. Opera helps me understand the personality of various instruments and how to put them in communication with one another. I can use this knowledge for later symphonies. Many people consider opera as the crown of culture. If music raises nations, then I will take that crown and wear it proudly on my head for Deutschland.

Instruments are the easy part. Composition is not terribly difficult either. It's like a challenging puzzle, one in which I design the picture. I coordinate a string of ideas into musical form. No idea is impossible for the great Louis to puzzle together. My art makes me feel like I am free.

The choices are limitless. I can create sounds that the world has never heard before. For this reason, I want to devote my life's work to human freedom since Music is freeing. I'm still developing my style, so I have a long road ahead.

Hence, my next pursuit is to have lessons with the revered and highly esteemed Joseph Haydn. I sent him several letters with no reply. I am sure he's heard of me by now. What musician wouldn't want to teach a protege? If Haydn had me as a student, all of Europe would be knocking at his door. I made that exact statement in my letters, multiple times. Alas, patience is a virtue. Or at least that's what I am told.

One day the world will praise my name with these great artists, and when that time comes, I will not be satisfied, for I must rise above peasant fanfare.

—Ludwig van Beethoven II

August 1790

Dear Success,

Ah, this title suits my journal better.

I've had several lessons with Joseph Haydn. It appears he retrieved his senses. I simply adore the man! Haydn shares my passion for symphonies. I cannot wait to develop my compositional skills with him! He is fortunate to have me.

—Ludwig Van Beethoven

August 1790

Dear Success,

I have this great idea for a symphony, a symphony to Napoleon Bonaparte! I got the inspiration from a previous note I wrote in this journal as a child: *"Maybe one day I can write a symphony! Or an opera grand enough for a real-life hero!"* I will take the best of both points and make a symphony for France's great hero. This is the perfect way for me to develop my philosophy of Music as freedom since Napoleon is the champion of freedom and fraternity.

Classical music is bound to pattern and structure; therefore, I will do something completely new. Something unheard of to the history of music. I will create the first symphony entirely centered on a persona, the persona of heroism. For I know of no other word to describe the First Consul of France. Bonaparte is so heroic that his title does not suit him. He is the greatest Roman Consul our world has ever seen. I have no melody line yet, as I am still playing with sounds in my head fit for this anthem to freedom. All I know for now is that I want Bonaparte's name written in large letters at the top of the director's score, and mine written in large letters at the bottom. I deserve to have my name written among the greats. The symphony needs no other text since history will remember my name as the hero of Music. My mission is to free Music from its classical parameters, just as the French revolution freed its brethren from the parameters of a monarchy.

—Ludwig van Beethoven

November 1790

Dear success,

The Bonaparte Symphony is published! I am so proud. It will bring tears to women's eyes and strength to the hearts of men.

—Ludwig van Beethoven

February 1791

Fiend! Fool! Fickle ferret!

I was blinded by my insolent adoration. Napoleon Bonaparte is no great Consul of Rome. How ashamed I am of esteeming him so! He's not even a consul anymore. The madman has crowned himself emperor. He is nothing more than an ordinary human being, the audacity! He has trampled all rights of men! Cut off Freedom's head and exchanged it for tyranny.

I am wallowing in embarrassment! How could he defy my intelligence so much that my Music could become polluted be his audacious tyranny?

Upon hearing this news, I rushed to my score and scribbled out any association of this fowl name with my own. I nearly tore my score apart in a fit of rage. Instead, I will rename my symphony *Eroica*, so the world may never forget the true persona of heroic freedom.

—Ludwig van Beethoven

May 1791

Dear Success,

I lost my inspiration since that recent incident which I shall not speak of. I turned to Haydn for help. I asked him where he finds his inspiration and he imparted his wisdom to me. I must recite Haydn's most sacred words, to the best of my recollection:

Haydn: "I find my inspiration in the mystery of Beauty. Beauty with a capital B since God is the source. For example, I can find a flower beautiful, but if I allow its beauty to penetrate me and take me somewhere beyond myself, then it is truly Beautiful. Music is like that. It can bring our hearts to God. Therefore, I am intentional about every note, every marking, and every cadence I write. If my Music can give the audience an experience that mirrors God's perfection then it will move them, and the audience shares in a deeper understanding of His great mystery. Recently, the flower I've been pondering is Schiller's poem, "Ode to Joy." Have you heard of it, Ludwig? In the first stanza, the beloved is referred to as,

'A spark of fire from Heaven.'

*As the reader, I can interpret this in my own way, and I see the beloved
as Music. Music is a pure spark from Heaven, a gift to the world of art. Schiller described the beloved as a 'magic power [which] binds together . . . where
all men emerge as brothers.' This is the power of Music, Ludwig. It creates
community and facilitates culture. You know something is Beautiful and from
God when it binds people together."*

I am glad I had this conversation with Haydn. Maybe I depended too
much on one human being to satisfy my inspiration. Turns out humans are
not reliable, since the one I shall not name has made himself a god. Beauty
is dependable. Beauty is always around us, and the joy in Schiller's poem
reminds me of this. But what if that's merely a sweet sentiment? I wonder
if the people pillaged by Bonaparte's warfare find any beauty in life. Surely
there must be something that keeps their hearts going in hope of Freedom.

I will never forget Haydn's words of wisdom. *"Ode to Joy"* is now my
favorite poem and I aspire to live by it as an artist.

—Ludwig van Beethoven

April 1797

Dear Success,

My good friend, Baron Gottfried van Swieten, diplomat of the Holy
Roman Empire, has provided me with accommodations to write music for
him. What an honor, I am so humbled! I well respect the man, but I had to
tell him not to assign dates to my art. He must understand that I compose
on my own time. I do not speak to the Music; it speaks to me. All good
things come in good time.

—Ludwig van Beethoven

April 1799

Dear Success,

I have enough money to support my poor family and to stand on my own as a musician. This accomplishment is unheard of! I've composed a lot of orchestral music, and my recent symphony is the crowning glory of my work thus far! Symphony No. 1 in C major. I dedicated it to Baron Gottfried van Swieten. It premiered a few days ago. The audience was bewildered with amazement. The moment I put my baton down, the concert hall fell into an enraptured silence. They knew not whether to stand, or applaud, or cry, for they had no idea that Music could express itself with so much conviction and emotion. All their answers were lost in a mystery where Music is the medium between spiritual and sensual worlds. It's moments like these when I know I am fulfilling my calling as an artist. My symphony was such a success in Vienna, that France and Italy are already calling my name. It made newspaper headlines across Europe. Grandfather would be proud.

—Ludwig van Beethoven

April 1799

Dear Success.

There are so many sounds that the human ear has not explored yet. Hence, my calling resonates with Schiller's, *"Ode to Joy."* I like the lines that say, *"True to heaven's mighty plan, / Brothers, run your course now, /Happy as a knight in victory."* I see how Music is calling my name on this path of victory. Freedom, fraternity, and joy, all championed in this poem as in my Music. To this divine inspiration, I attribute my kind regards to Joseph Haydn. However, I am noticing that my style is becoming more my own.

Any musician who lives solely by the rules of modality is wasting the fullness of his talent. Why does Music always have to sound perfect as God is perfect? The human experience is imperfect like the dissonances that certain composers avoid. I will use regular dissonance to make my Music more relatable to the audience. I will explore the mysteries of Music that are yet untouched by mankind.

—Ludwig van Beethoven

February 1800

Dear Sorrow,

The strangest thing happened today. I told myself I was making it up, but my anxieties were racing out of control. I was playing my piano, as I do to start off every morning. Nothing unusual, till the highest register had a distant twangy sound. I tore my piano apart inside and out. It sounded like I dropped a metal nib inside it - as I've done before – but I found it on my feather pen where I left it. I cannot describe the sound properly, like it was on some far away hill. I then placed my hands on the keys again and closed my eyes. To my horror, I could not distinguish between C8 and B7. How can that be? I have perfect pitch. At that point, I ran to my violin and played scales. Everything sounded normal until A7. I rosined my bow and wiped the strings. Still the note lost its sweetness.

I hope this is only temporary.

I am too young to lose my hearing.

—Ludwig van Beethoven

March 1800

Dear Success,

My piano concerto in E-flat minor was performed at the Hoftheater! Prince Lichnowsky granted me an annual retaining fee for future commissions.

—Ludwig van Beethoven

November 1800

My hearing is much worse.

March 1801

I thought it would be well over by now.

July 1801

Still no sign of recovery.

December 1801

There will be hope next year.

January 1802

C5, where are you?

May 1802

WHY ME? Why

November 1802

Dear Sorrow,

I am not sure why the Vienna String Quartet has rallied against me!

I wrote a string quartet for Razumovsky, the Russian ambassador of Vienna, in F Major. He is a great friend and patron of mine; I was also presented with an opportunity to conduct the Vienna Quartet. What an honor to lead my own music!

To my great dismay, the musicians lacked the passion I intended for this piece. I kept yelling at them to light a fire in their souls. If they do not know what passion is, it is my job as the conductor and composer to scare it into them. They not only lacked passion, but dynamics as well. I simply could not hear them. I know this is not on me. What sort of lazy ferrets call themselves musicians if they have no desire to feel the music? Problem number one is they lacked any cognitive understanding of music.

I composed the piece with Russian influence for my good friend. But the lead violinist had the audacity to tell me I put the accents in the wrong places! Like he knows anything about culture! The cellist complained next. *"Excuse me Kapellmeister Beethoven, but I am playing the same note far too many times."* I would have informed him that it was to embody the humor of Razumovsky, but few musicians know what it means to have music represent a persona. I may have lost control of my anger at that point. To be fair, I did try to bestow mercy on their stupidity. I lifted my baton to conduct the next section, in an attempt to ignore it. He then threw my music on the ground. My music! In complete defiance.

I punched his cello. He deserved it. There might be a hole in the upper right side of its wooden face. By now, the whole instrument probably caved-in on itself. I hope the soundpost gets dislodged. Anyway, this is not my fault. They did not have to go on strike! Who is better to conduct my own work than myself? They could have played louder at the very least.

Now my false reputation as a madman precedes me. All the time, people misinterpret my passion for rage. And they misinterpret my social distance as insanity. I did not choose to have ears that make life difficult.

Life is so hard for me.

—Ludwig van Beethoven

December 1810

Dear Solitude,

I have failed to keep you company, my diary and closest friend.

I've been falling in and out of drunkenness this last decade. I still compose and get bursts of creativity. But my main patron, Prince Lichnowsky, went bankrupt years ago. I write music only to make a few coins, and to express my sorrows in a world that otherwise neglects to hear my pain.

No one can know that I am nearly deaf. I have to pretend that I am worthy of my great title since my talent is so highly esteemed. If Vienna were to find out about my disability, I would be replaced with a less talented and more proficient composer. No one understands. Every performance is a show for me rather than an experience. It breaks my heart not to hear what I create. I'm so exhausted from wearing a mask all the time! No one speaks my language. I have nothing but music, and even then, I rely more on the sounds I imagine in my head than reality. I am afraid of what people will think if they find out that the great Ludwig van Beethoven is disabled. They might send me to an asylum where my artistic pursuits would be restricted. No, I prefer my own solitude to that. Only the claw marks on my piano and the pages of this diary can carry my secret.

—Ludwig van Beethoven

February 1811

I've accepted my reality.

March 1811

It can't possibly get worse after this. I am sure of it.

October 1811

How can this be?! I can hardly hear my fingers play the keys!
They slither across the piano like a phantom of my former self.
Not one. Single. Sound.

November 1811

Dear Success,

It might help to exaggerate dynamics. I will use this trick in my compositions from now on. If I make harsh dynamic changes, it will be easier for me to follow scores when I conduct. It will help me feel the sound waves better and see the motion of musicians as they shift from ff and pp. This way I have more to rely on than the sounds I imagine in my head.

—Ludwig van Beethoven

December 1811

I AM SO DONE. I AM SO DONE WITH LIFE.

Everyone wrongs me. All I see are glares and snarls that imply I'm too malevolent and stubborn to talk to. If I could hear, I would have more to say. Instead, all people see is my rage. They fail to ask why I am so angry all the time. It's completely unfair! I can't even ask people to speak up, or they will know. I am a slave to the music in my head, to shadows I inscribe, with no freedom to hear. My success is built on fraudulence.

—Ludwig van Beethoven

January 1812

Dear Solitude,

Why must you love me so much? I despise you! I try to rid myself of your nasty odor, like that of an abandoned corpse. I dispel the sound of your voice from my ears, but you are all I hear: Nothing. Very little. No one but Solitude. Every time I reject you, I am further bound by you, further rejected. An outcast. A nobody. Lost in a world I do not belong to.

I scream to the heavens. WHY ME? And I hear no reply. Does anyone hear me? Or see the depths of my agony? Am I even seen?—Only known for my music which I cannot hear. I deserve to hear it. Me! More than anyone else. It's MY music. I long from the very depths of my being to identify with its Beauty.

Why must you befriend me? Why must you pretend to understand? I do not choose isolation because I love you, I choose it out of necessity. I want my old self back. I want human warmth. I want someone out there to understand me or to save me. Simply someone to talk to. I cannot even communicate. I am so lost. I desire so much but have so little. I am little. Why am I such scum? You pretend to be my friend, Solitude, but you deepen my agony like a dagger. You use my impairment for your own gain. Alcohol is a dearer friend than you.

I wish my mother never bore me.

—Yours not truly,
Ludwig van Beethoven.

February 1812

A poem to commemorate my defeats:

Life is-a scare crow
Skin bone-and thread.
Lost in-a plateau
Un-moved nor fed.

Here I go . . .
Highly exulted

This is-so dreadful
I want-to die.

Existence is too rotten. I no longer have pride in my musical accomplishments. The only thing that keeps me going is the hope that someone might hear my music and understand my emotions. Unlike Schiller's, "*Ode to Joy*," this poem is real. It doesn't have a misperceived notion that joy is attainable. It has a nice rhythm to it as well. I need to write a third movement for my seventh symphony, so I'll use this as inspiration for the funeral march, a tribute to my desired death.

—Ludwig van Beethoven

May 1815

I see I have neglected my diary for a few years. The whole point of it was to record my life successes. When I lost my aim, I lost all motivation to continue writing. Now I have something to share, and I'm still trying to process it. I'll make a feeble attempt:

Dear Savior,

My angel, whomever You may be. I know not what eternal Beauty hides your face, nor why you've called me from the depths of despair. Allow me to write down the events I want never to forget:

Last night I was recovering from a drunken stupor. I awoke to find myself on a park bench. The dream I had awoken from felt real. There's no way I could have conjured it on my own, nor recalled it enough to write the story. The dream was nothing short of miraculous.

I found myself face-to-face with a muzzle. Before I could see who had the audacity to hold me at gunpoint, my whole life flashed before my eyes. My successes, my failures, my aims, and pursuits. Who is Ludwig van Beethoven? Why is there so much regret? Have I lived a worthy life? I'm not ready to die...

One shot obliterated my deaf ears. Then a second, and a third. Each missing my head. Scared . . . shaking . . . scattered . . . I gathered enough courage to focus my eyes on the man who wished death upon me. It was me. I found he was myself, staring back as if in a mirror. I looked into his eyes—my eyes. There was anger and hatred (no surprise). Yet deeper than that, I saw something more than a will to live. Ah, how can the visual expression of one's own soul be put into words? While my finger clinged to the trigger for relief, I saw in the mirror of my eyes a spark, a pure enjoyment of life. Like a single note that starts a symphony. Beauty born from nothing. Where does it come from? A call to create, to keep living for Beauty's sake.

I dropped the gun. My life was free.

Then in this miraculous dream, I heard a trumpet blare in reply to that single note. It wasn't like the music I imagine in my head, for it was the most real sound I've heard in years! Its gift strengthened my heart as if a fiery hearth were lit from within. My desire to create soared above the clangs of death and into the stars of the sky. Amid the chaos sang a voice above and beyond me, beautiful and angelic as a sweet soprano heroine: "There must live a loving father. / Do you kneel down low, you millions? / Do you see your maker, world? / Search for Him above the stars, / Above the stars he must be living." I recognized the lyrics from Shiller's "Ode to Joy." The one that inspired my vocation in Music when I was younger. I wondered at the universe. What is joy? How can I find it? What must I do?

While this was all but a dream—perhaps a vision from some Divine Aid—I felt no less that I had narrowly escaped death.

I awoke from the park bench. The soprano and trumpet duet had come to an end and its resonance mingled with the rising sun. The sky, a pink and orange sea of mystery that raised me from the ashes. An enjoyment of life. The mystery of Beauty like the Music I write. My gaze lost itself to the distant rolling hills. A shepherd guarded his sheep in the lush-green pastures beyond. Protected from harm, he is their Savior. It reminded me of the Pastoral Symphony I wrote over a decade ago and its sweet dance-like melody inspired a hope inside me that maybe joy isn't some false perception in life. I could not have conjured that expression completely on my own, for its joy must have come from somewhere. Something? Someone? How else would I know how to compose Music that brings joy to my audience? Where does that knowledge come from? It is not completely foreign to me. Joy is a part of the human experience, after all. I've simply lost my way in recent years.

Dear Solitude,

I cannot rid the world of my existence. I have more to say in my Music. Thank you for showing me this.

—Ludwig van Beethoven

June 1816

Dear Sorrow,

My brother Kasper died unexpectedly of a heart-attack this morning. He left his son Karl and a widow behind. I took little care of my brother during his short lifetime. Therefore, I do not feel like I've lost someone, but I regret the friend I could have had. I must return to Bonn for the funeral.

—Ludwig van Beethoven

July 1816

Dear Solitude,

I'm back in the place of my birth. I took a lovely walk along the Rhine to recollect myself after the funeral. The Rhine's beauty seemed to wind on forever. What secrets were whispered from its divine depths? Its surface glimmered with flecks of light and hope. Surrounded by grey clouds. The type of hope that can only be found in a sea of sorrow. Water sings of life. Was the Rhine dead inside, or was it just my reflection? Where was the river going?

Where am I going?

I used to walk along the Rhine with my grandfather as a child. He was the only family member I felt kinship with. I despised my father. He loved alcohol more than me. A pathetic excuse for a man. I've spent my life trying to be the exact opposite of him.

I HATE MYSELF! I depend on the same substance that tore my family apart.

Am I a pathetic excuse for a man?

And what about the rest of my family? They shun me. I know not why, but I cannot stand to live like this anymore. I am lonely. I have no family. I must do something. Something, Does the river know? I think it whispered for me to stay in Bonn a little longer.

—Ludwig van Beethoven

August 1816

Dear Solitude,

All my life, I've despised my brother Johan who was named after my father. I lost one brother who I never took the time to know, so I wrote a letter of apology to his continental wife. I apologized for all the racial and sexual slurs I've ever spoken to her. I hope to make amends. If she loves me, then Johan will surely come around and love me too. After all, Schiller's poem says that all men are brothers, and I have denied myself of this fundamental goodness in life.

—Ludwig van Beethoven

September 1816

Dear Solitude,

As for my other sister-in-law, I am the new guardian of her son, Karl. I've saved him from the clutches of this poor unfortunate drunken widow. She must understand I have all good intentions for the boy. I sent Karl to an institute under the direction of Giannatsio de Rio so he may learn music. He will turn into a protege just like myself at that age. I hope one day Karl will want me to be his father-figure.

—Ludwig van Beethoven

October 1818

Dear Sorrow,

Karl's mother brought an action against me and won the case. He moved back in with her. That boy was nothing but trouble anyway. Even the institute couldn't put up with the dung heap that is Karl's god-awful behavior, I put so much hope in that boy! I gave him everything, including an esteemed education. And while I was legally responsible for Karl these last few years, he gave me hell. He constantly ran away from me. I thought I could create a sense of family, but that mother—if I should even call her that—wants nothing to do with me. I have no idea why she thinks I have an unruly temper. She said I am not good for the boy's wellbeing. Even if that were true, it's no reason to call an action against me.

I feel like there is a physical thorn in my heart. The court case and recent loss of Karl has a hammer banging at my skull. To remedy this, I try to remind myself that my quality of life has gone up in his absence. While I miss Karl, I am freed from the constant issues I have to problem solve for him. I cannot decide if the house is too quiet or just enough quiet.

—Ludwig van Beethoven

November 1818

Dear Solitude,

I had to stop conducting in the middle of a concert. I couldn't hear a thing. My ears are completely shot. I am home now and still shaking out of sheer embarrassment. I had to stop the orchestra without explanation, walk past the audience, and leave like nothing was unusual. I felt in that moment like the ground had left my feet and I am still falling . . .

January 1822

Dear Solitude, my friend,

I'm afraid I neglected you because I've been so busy. The last season of life was one of despair, but there's also been a sense of success. Busyness is a better distraction than alcohol. And I am tired of people accusing me of being an unruly man, stubborn, difficult to deal with, and irritable. I've been working on myself. Now there is no ground for simple-minded opinions! Sober Louis is a new Louis. A new season in life.

Also! I've returned from seeing my Missa Solemnis performed at St. Cassius and Florentius. It was such a success that I've already been commissioned to write another one. I'm thinking in C minor next time. I say "success" because it raised my heart to the Divine. I could feel it. The whole congregation was transposed into brotherly communion and raised to the source of Beauty.

—Ludwig van Beethoven

February 1823

Dear Solitude,

I submitted my Missa Solemnis in C minor to the publisher and the most miraculous thing happened on my way home. Here, in the middle of winter, I discovered a single rose still holding onto life. How I didn't notice it before, I will never know. It was white like snow, and its fragrance was one of hope. This rose is the epitome of life. For by some mystery, the Rose is built upon thorns. It must grow in pain, yet the pain cannot tarnish its Beauty. Its pedals rotate in a circular motion around a fixed point – a desire to be centered in something beyond oneself that is greater than and still part of. For this reason, my sweet little rose held on through the cold winter. Now it adorns my dining room table. It gives me inspiration for my greatest work of all time, but I will keep it as a surprise for you, my sweet Solitude.

—Ludwig van Beethoven

August 1824

Dear Solitude,

Alas, I need not over-explain myself to you, for you are always with me and you've heard it all before. You know how much it pains me that I cannot listen to my own Music. Like bolts of lightning that travel through my ears to paralyze my heart. Over and over again.

My nineth symphony is the surprise I have for you. It's the masterpiece of Freedom embodied in Music. I used Schiller's poem as the text for the world's first ever choral symphony. I wonder what my last movement with the "Ode to Joy" would sound like if I could hear. It's the greatest work of my genius. I composed the melody to be broken and interrupted in unexpected places by the contrabasses, violincellos, bassoons, and trombones. This creates a dark texture like the pain of existence, constantly distracting one from the Goodness of life. Joy triumphs in the end. I have the melody restarted in unison with the whole symphony, then freed once more from its constraints with 100 choristers who join in singing the lyrics of Schiller's poem. The grand ending will bring my audience to contemplate what Freedom is so they may remember who they are, regardless of any pain in their personal lives. I hope to bring my audience to a place where impairment has no voice except to transport one's soul to the Divine, like my Rose in winter.

I cannot wait to see the reaction of my first audience after they experience my ninth symphony. It will be like nothing that has ever been heard or imagined before.

Thank you, Solitude, for being the ears to my symphony.

Yours truly,
—Ludwig van Beethoven

July 1824

Dear Solitude,

Karl's mother wrote to me for support. She needs to be relieved of her duties as a widow and mother for an unknown time. Now I can have my nephew back, the closest thing I ever had to a son. I pray to heaven that I can forgive him of all his craziness and be the man he needs in his life. I am preparing my house for his arrival.

—Ludwig van Beethoven

August 1824

Dear Solitude,

After hearing my "Ode to Joy," King Louis XVIII awarded me a gold medal for my contribution to European culture.

—Ludwig van Beethoven

Dear reader,

Most music historians consider Beethoven as the turning point between the classical and romantic era. Romantic music is similar to classical music, but is centered more on self-expression, where most classical composers created patterns to mirror the perfection of God. Beethoven was nominally Catholic, and his sense of God was more as a transcendent Beauty than as a practiced faith. Beethoven is known as the father of romantic music because his philosophy is combined with a newer one, one of the adamant self-expressions that allowed him to experiment with new sounds in complex harmony and texture. In this way, romantic music is highly expressive as it relates the artist's inner life to the world around them.

Beethoven is known for his unruly temper and stubborn behavior, as described in written accounts and portraits. My piece focuses more on his arrogance, as I imagine it. These attributes made Beethoven difficult to work with. Nevertheless, he was one of the few artists to be well appreciated in his lifetime. Beethoven's story is inspiring due to the sheer influence he had on music despite his hearing loss. I chose to highlight this struggle to imagine how it may have helped him grow as a person. Beethoven also faced great mental health struggles. Some historians and musicians suspect he struggled with narcissism; others suspect bipolar disorder. During one period of his life, Beethoven considered suicide. In a written account of Beethoven's thoughts on the matter, his last sentence illudes to a sense of hope. He wrote, "it seemed to me impossible to leave the world until I had brought forth all that I felt was within me," (The Heiligenstadt Testament). This desire to bring his inner expression into the world is what made Beethoven's music a revolution of self-expression. Throughout his life, Beethoven wrote music to explore what freedom sounds like. His unique intelligence allowed him to imagine every instrument in his head with all the complex harmonies of his symphonies. Even with his impairment, Beethoven knew the symphony well enough to expand its size, traditional techniques, and musical complexity.

Beethoven's symphonies are among the most well-known, due to the timeless beauty and relatability of his work. His most influential piece is

Symphony No. 9 in D minor, which features Schiller's "Ode to Joy" in the world's first ever choral symphony. Its sentiments of freedom, fraternity, and joy have been a source of inspiration against war and depression throughout the centuries. It inspired the philosophies of later composers, including the famous German composer, Gustav Mahler, who composed the Resurrection Symphony. Like Beethoven's Nineth, his is a choral symphony on the philosophy of Freedom, although Mauler composed it from the Christian definition of Freedom found in Jesus Christ. Moreover, Beethoven's Nineth Symphony was used days after the fall of the Berlin Wall. Leonard Bernstein conducted the symphony in West Germany and in the liberated East Germany. Musicians from both sides performed together as brothers once again, which relates to Schiller's emphasis on fraternity. To celebrate this occasion, Bernstein changed the title. He advertised it as the "Ode an die Freiheit," the *Ode to Freedom,* instead of the "Ode to Joy." In place of the original text, the choir exchanged the word "joy" for "freedom." Beethoven's Ninth Symphony is still played across the world to celebrate occasions, and in my hometown, it is performed to ring-in the New Year.

SOURCES

Beethoven, Ludwig van. *The Heiligenstadt Testament.* Frankfort: Whippoorwill, 1982.

Beethoven, Ludwig van, and Michael Hamburger. *Beethoven: Letters, Journals and Conversations.* London: Thames and Hudson, 1992.

Burkholder, J., Donald Grout, and C. Palisca. *History of Western Music.* New York: Norton, 2019.

Solomon, Maynard. *Beethoven.* London: Macmillan, 1977.

Sagittae Angelorum

Short Stories—V

Home Bound

by Lucas Smith

The depressurizing oxygen conduits aggressively hissed and violently smoked around the entrance ramp as it opened to the gray landing zone. Upon making contact, workers armed with magnetic loaders began moving cargo crates from the dock to the ship, ship to the dock, all with industrial speed and precision. Red, blue, yellow, and green striped crates, designating their contents, whizzed to-and-fro, empties being placed here, incoming products there. A leather-clad, scruffy redhead with an unkept beard and piercing green eyes stood in the loading bay of the landed transport shuttle with a coffee in hand. He watched red dust being blown gently over the star port: dozens of other crafts were having their contents also moved with lightening pace.

They remained encased in a large transparent dome, artificial lights illuminating it mysteriously from the base of the construct, while the rest was from buildings, machinery, and workers. Beyond lay a red desert of rock and dust, spotted with the occasional antenna array for communications. Other large domes spotted the horizon, the metropolitan centers that now dotted Mars.

He sipped his coffee. The eeriness of this planet never was lost on him; only a couple centuries ago this was considered imaginary, but here he found himself, a delivery boy for the Mars colony. A man with a clip board made his way towards his spot on the ramp. He downed the last bit of his coffee and jumped down to meet him.

"Afternoon Dolan," the man with the board called out over the sound of electric engines and jostling cargo. The dark sky of the lonely planet shimmered with starlight above.

"Same to you Hester," Dolan said grabbing Hester's free hand. "Signature?" He said pointing to the clipboard. Dolan had run this delivery more times than he could count, it had become almost automatic at this point, and this more personal interaction with Hester was out of the ordinary.

"Yeah, just wanted to run a few things over with you first before I send you off for a well-deserved break, you mind?" Hester gestured to his office behind him to the side of the platform. "I'll refill your coffee while we are at it." Dolan thought of how he really needed to replace his coffee machine on board the *East Chaser*.

"Sure thing," Dolan approved, "I got time." Making their way towards the office, Dolan found himself staring off into the night sky that harkened back to his childhood evenings in open fields, lost in the endlessness of the heavens.

As Hester punched some buttons on a tarnished coffee machine, the machine hummed and began to spit out the dark liquid. "Thanks for taking some time aside here to talk, you are a hard-working lifter," Hester gestured towards the mug in Dolan's hand with a nod and extended arm. Dolan handed his dented thermos to him. The flattery was noted in Hester's comments: Dolan knew something was going to be asked of him.

The two men sat down in stationary chairs at a desk. The office was compact and stacks of supposedly ordered forms sat on tables and chairs that lined the room. Hester's desk equally lacked such order; cups, wire, paper, empty pens, and more miscellaneous office gear lay strewn about. Amid the chaos, one item hung perfectly on the back corner wall: a crucifix.

"How's business Hester? Keeping her afloat? I know the last quarter was hard with tensions boiling." A U.N. meeting last month was working on a document attempting to define the nations of Mars, but strife between counties who had invested in settling the Red Planet were pushing back, attempting to claim these 'Red Colonies' as additions to their pre-existing states. Military violence had been avoided so far, but whispers were forming of something behind the scenes.

Hester glanced distractedly at the closed windows and locked door behind Dolan. "Hey Dolan," Hester said ignoring the questions, "I have a favour to ask that is off the books." Dolan had been offered under the table deals before, turning them down to avoid unwanted stress, he had enough of that just making sure he could keep the *East Chaser* moving from point A to B. Dolan glanced at the crucifix that felt uncomfortably present in his peripheral vision.

"I'll hear you out, but I can't make any promises," Dolan replied. The coffee had finished, but the conversation held Dolan to his chair with force, the crucifix inviting him to remain seated.

Hester opened a drawer in a side cabinet and pulled out a manila envelope, placing it in front of Dolan. The folder was labelled *Shining Light*. Dolan pulled in closer.

"I trust your character Dolan, you are a respectable man, more than most who pull through my port." Hester shifted in his seat leaning closer. "She just needs to get to Earth, the coordinates are in the folder, I don't trust anyone else with this and I wouldn't dare send her with anyone else." Dolan interjected,

"She? Her? What is going on here?" Dolan pushed the document back, "Slave? Prostitute? This is out of line!" as his voice raised, he began to get up.

"She's a nun!" Hester blurted with desperation. Dolan froze, the crucifix now demanding his attention, piercing him. "Please, she needs to get out of here, no one can know." Dolan did not know what came over him. A new immediacy took root in his mind, no longer of washing his hands of this matter but one of taking this upon himself to see through. There seemed to be only one response he could muster.

"When can we leave?"

"She is hiding on site; she can be ready in fifteen."

"I'll be on the ship." Dolan walked out of the office, folder in hand.

As the fifteen-minute window was coming to a close, Dolan had to catch his wandering anxious thoughts as they strayed into the desolate Mar's landscape that stretched out beyond the dome. Dolan was sitting, unsettled in his cockpit. Visions of the crucifix fixed to the wall rattled around his mind. The aroma of incense was faintly present, subtle Gregorian chant from his youth greeted his minds ear, greens, whites, reds . . . the sensations of a life he thought behind him came knocking on the door of the present.

A proximity sensor sprouted to life accompanied by the sound of static, interrupting his aimless reflections. Dolan leaned close to see if his 'cargo' was ready for pick up. A dark figure, hooded from his perspective, stood patiently outside the back hatch, a single brown suitcase in hand. Grabbing a nearby handgun, just in case this was a setup, Dolan made his way to the hatch after disengaging the sensor. He walked towards the aft of the *East Chaser*, punched in the password, and then hit a red blinking button to open the rear hatch.

With a quick rapid burst of hissing, the hatch ramp extended, the figure stood motionless as she noticed the gun in his right hand. Dolan found himself faced by a familiar yet foreign style that had long since escaped his memory, but the words arose as if they had never fallen asleep:

"Benedictine?" Dolan asked.

The girl with the black hood with white veil sought a space for her lone possession, her suitcase that seemed practically empty. As Dolan began to prep for take-off, few words except for pointing out seating and cargo space had passed between. Before the silence could suffocate him, Dolan spoke up from his pilot seat.

"What do you go by miss?" She paused for a moment before speaking, as if reflecting and soaking in the question in its entirety.

"Sister Athena" she replied timidly, returning the eye contact that Dolan had extended. Her soft green eyes met his faded brown eyes, hers expressing a peace that lay just behind them, Dolan's conveying a fatigue that had accumulated over many years. "I should like to know yours as well," Athena went on, shifting slightly in her seat, "Though, I am not sure if in your line of work you prefer to keep such things confidential." She rested her hands in her lap as she sat composed on a small table and chair that Dolan used for meals, papers, and the occasional unintentional nap.

"No mysteries on my end, just a cargo hauler, nothing fancy or under wraps. Names Dolan." The tension began evaporated with a growing familiarity and authenticity coming to form that had never made itself known on the bridge nor bulkhead of this average shipping container of a star ship. The gray of the walls seem to lift to a lighter hew knowing that something precious now lay within it.

With the green light for lift off being given from Hester, Dolan pitched the *East Chaser* up and off the landing pad, the rumbling from the four main boosters rattling anything not tied down on board. Sister Athena had one hand clutching the fixed table, the other a crucifix that lay under her habit. Dolan rotated the ship toward the dome and moved forward to begin departure. A static voice came across the comms.

"Dolan," Hester said through the static, "thank you again." Dolan looked down at the comms controls, a blinking light showing it was broadcasting. A comfort rolled over him, a confirmation that this was what he needed to do; no, that this was what he was meant to do.

"I'll see you again Hester, keep well up here." Due to the orbits of the Earth and Mars, constant travel was not possible. The longer years of Mars led to different orbital periods, hiding the Red Planet behind the blazing Sun for almost a year, isolating the colony from her significant other.

A section of the dome opened and released the *East Chaser* to begin her voyage home. Engaging the sub-light engines as they left orbit, the red dot punctuated with human settlements faded into the inky blackness of space behind them.

"Ever been up here, Athena?" Dolan asked over his shoulder.

"Never." Athena said in awe looking through the front window shield from her seat.

"You may want to hold on extra tight for a moment." Dolan flipped a myriad of switches, punching buttons here and there for course settings and speed controls. Finally, he grabbed a leaver and pushed it forward. The stars began to elongate and turned to beams of dazzling light. The force of acceleration pushed Dolan and Athena into their seats. Dolan overheard a faint whisper from the nun as they began whizzing through the cosmos:

"Pater noster, qui es in cœlis . . . "

Dolan finished checking over the controls as the beams of stars created a funnel before them that whisked the craft closer to her destination. The trip would be no less then twelve hours, so Dolan opened the folder he had received from Hester and scanned the documents.

"So, you are a first-generation Martian?" Dolan asked Athena, raising the document in gesture. "Why leave? It's the dream of millions to one day immigrate to Mars."

Athena paused.

"What does that planet make you feel like?" Athena asked softly at last.

Dolan paused.

The red rock, dusty sky, and desolate landscape crept into his mind. He realized that even though he had stood on what remained so far beyond humanities reach for so many generations, Mars remained barren. Barren except for the jewels of her night skies. For that lonely planet, the crown of her beauty was that of leaving man to stand and stare at what lay beyond.

"Alone. Dreadfully alone." Dolan responded. He continued to look through the documents. Pages of family records, birth certificate identifying her as early twenties, and a baptismal record along with admission into the Benedictine's.

Standing up from his seat, Dolan moved into the section of the ship where Athena sat in quiet contemplation. He pulled up a chair and sat near her. Her serenity was calming and gave confidence that he could ask her questions.

"Where am I taking you, Athena?" Dolan realized he had accepted this mission with little knowledge except a tugging at his inner conscience.

"Rome." She said simply. "The Vatican to be specific." The invoking of that ancient name cast a weight upon the *East Chaser* that equaled a large haul of supplies. With that name came crashing in the rich past with all her twists, turns, wars, and peacetimes. The smell of incense burned once more in Dolan's mind along with the image of a dove descending on a man robbed in white standing upon St. Peter's.

Athena noticed the churning of memories in Dolan's eyes.

"I miss history," she almost whispered. "I can sense that as well," Dolan nodded in agreement.

"I miss the connection," Dolan reflected, "the sense that what I do is plugged into something larger, something valuable. . ." He trailed off into thoughts of his youth, attending a Christian school, reading ancient texts that had a tinge of the present laced through out, then going home to watch the space port from his window, with small ships launching into the dark night. Athena looked at Dolan with compassion.

"I too miss the feeling of continuity with one's family," She turned more to face the sullen face of her pilot, "When I joined the order of Benedict, I felt both home yet lost. The Martian soil felt like the dirt that Christ wrote in with his own hand, something containing a lost mystery." She reached again for the concealed crucifix and squeezed. "Christ says what does it profit a man to gain the world but lose his soul? I feel I have lost the world and my soul by being so far from the very dirt in which my Savior walked, cried, and bled. I long to be closer. I do not wish to be tied to the world, yet I feel that earth is not just another planet, a pale blue dot in the night sky." A tear fell down her face, "It was on that dot that God became man." A second tear joined the first, contained within it a love that Dolan had only a faint recollection of from his youth.

Within that stream of true confession, a weeping for a far-away lover, Dolan saw with clear sight the last Mass he attended. He had been confused, angry, vindictive. Yet he remembered weeping despite this cocktail of darkness that swirled deep in his heart. Deeper still there was a voice that remained, a whisper, *I can wait my son. I will not leave you.* At the time, Dolan wrote this voice off as a trick of his own mind, a mind that lay confused in the darkness of the past and her errors. Now Dolan sat face to face with that voice made manifest once more. His running had come full circle.

Athena looked at Dolan, wiping the tear from her eye, and noticed that Dolan had also begun weeping. It was in that place they sat for the whole journey, speaking of those things that the heart seeks fervently: of joy, longing, family, the past, and the beauty of the future.

Snowflakes danced in the air as Dolan and Athena stepped off the *East Chaser*, her engines slowly coming to a stop after the voyage. They had touched down at two in the morning on Christmas day. The lights of that immortal city glowed as the white snow gently settled among the Churches and stone streets. The supernatural mural radiated sublime peace in all directions. It was as if the city itself extended a warm hug that enveloped their whole being, an embrace made of a thousand generations.

They boarded a taxi that smelled of old smoke and age. The driver, an Italian of many years wearing thin glasses and a white dress shirt, smiled as they sat down.

"To St. Peter's please," Dolan said with both a great fatigue and yet also a primordial joy, "and Merry Christmas."

"*Si, signore, Buon Natale!*" replied the driver with equal joy. The vehicle lurched forward in the snow-dusted streets.

Athena stared out the windows of that small taxi with more wonder than that of the *East Chaser*. It was as if the lights that dotted the streets themselves became the fires of the heavens that raced by them in beams as they drove the silent streets of the morning. The edifices of historic architecture captured the imagination like that of a nebula, the intricacies drawing one deeper into the mystery of the world that surrounded them. The majestic Basilicas of St. Paul Outside-the-Walls, St. John Lateran, St. Mary Major, and finally, St. Peter's impressed upon Dolan and Athena the reality of reality itself. They stepped out of the cab into the square of Saint Peter's.

They stood in the silence of that morning, soaking in the gravity of their surroundings. Athena turned and embraced Dolan with tears rolling down her face and awe in her eyes.

"Thank you, Dolan, thank you." She wept with the joy one has at meeting family for the first time after decades apart. Dolan embraced her in return.

"I," Dolan started, the glow of the streetlights and the Basilica before him standing constant and sublime, "I think I'm home."

About the Authors

JEREMY JOOSTEN spent his childhood fighting monsters with his brothers in his backyard. Preoccupied with the idea of being a superhero or an actor, Jeremy had to grow up and went to public school for much of his life. He studies Business and Psychology at Trinity Western University and was elected student association president for the 2023–2024. Jeremy enjoys the look on people's faces when they discover that he writes poetry, short stories, and plays.

JOELLE JOOSTEN was raised in Seattle, Washington, the eldest of six siblings, in a multi-racial and devout Catholic family. Joelle is a twin with adopted siblings from Georgia, Guatemala, and Inner Mongolia. She appreciates theater and has been involved in music with the Tacoma Youth Symphony and Saint James Cathedral choir. Joelle writes with God's grace in mind reflecting on the human condition and forgiveness. Joelle is currently studying Primary Education in British Columbia.

DOMINIC NOOTEBOS was born in Langley, British Columbia where he grew up in a Catholic family of eight. Dominic's provocative writing, at times playful poetry, at other times gothic romances, delight and disturb the mind and heart. Besides honing his creative craft, Dominic is fascinated by computer sciences. But when not staring at a screen, Dominic plays classical music on the piano or strums new cords on his guitar.

LUCAS SMITH is a Vancouver, BC, city kid turned Abbotsford country boy. His one adventure out of Canada landed him on a mission trip in Nicaragua, fueling his love of God and neighbor. Lucas's writing leads his audience to stop and reflect on what he calls, "the in-between moments" of life. His commitment to Track & Field as well as Education has opened Lucas to the realities of life and faith.

Manufactured by Amazon.ca
Acheson, AB